HOW TO RUIN YOUR LIFE IN 140 CHARACTERS OR LESS

G. J. CRESPO

© 2021 by G. J. Crespo

rved.

ook may be reproduced in any form or by any electronic or
s, including information storage and retrieval systems, without
from the author, except for the use of brief quotations in a

design by Penelope McDonald

In memory of my mother-in-law, Marilyn, who loved children, animals, and most of all, her family, and who always had a kind word and a purse full of chocolate for anyone she met.

THURSDAY NIGHT

JTMonahan @JTMonahan 8 May
@SarahMcKay aka Ms McKay your jokes are lame you dress like an old lady I hate you and your f-ing math class what moron hired you #yousuck

HellionHernandez @HellionHernandez 8 May
@JTMonahan Nice use of social media.

JTMonahan @JTMonahan 8 May
@HellionHernandez nobody asked you loser

ONE
FRIDAY MORNING

I SHOULD HAVE KNOWN BETTER when my girlfriend Maddie told me *I had to* have a Twitter account. I also should have known better when she copied down my password; especially after she was forced to delete all of her social media accounts last fall. But my being a total dumb-ass doesn't excuse her from hijacking my account. My being a total dumb-ass does explain why I'm following Ms. Deon down the hall to in-school suspension.

Ms. Deon stops outside of Room 114 and says, "You're the only student in here today, so I had to scramble to find somebody to watch you. Mr. Watson should be here shortly." She opens the door and turns the lights on.

I take a couple of steps in and look around. It's the only classroom I've ever seen that didn't have windows. A couple of the fluorescent lights flicker and buzz and it smells a little musty. The way other kids describe it, I was expecting chains bolted to the walls and a rotting corpse in the corner.

Ms. Deon says, "Let's see, Mr. Watson will bring you down

to the cafeteria for lunch, but you'll eat here. Report here on Monday instead of your homeroom. I'll let your teachers know where you are and they'll arrange to get your assignments to you." She stops for a second. "I already told you no track meets or practice with the team while you're in suspension. I think that's about it." We wait and I stare at my shoes, the desks, anything to avoid the disappointment on her face. This is so humiliating. I never get in trouble. My phone buzzes twice in my pocket, but I don't dare take it out.

Mr. Watson, aka Jake, the athletic trainer, shows up out of breath and sweating. "Sorry. One of the juniors got beaned by a softball and I had to make sure he was okay."

Ms. Deon smiles and says, "Not a problem," and turns to me. "Any questions?"

"Can I go to my locker? All I have with me is my physics book."

"Sure. Mr. Watson can escort you." She stops in the doorway. "I almost forgot, no calls or texting. You can either leave your phone in your locker or Mr. Watson will hold it until the end of the day."

"Can I use it to take the tweet down?"

She nods and says, "Turn it in when you're done."

We do a locker run and my phone buzzes twice more before we get back to Room 114. I take a seat a safe distance from Jake and pull my phone out of my pocket. All four messages are from Maddie.

Im bored

Trish said you got called to deons office

Are you in trouble

Where r u

I don't respond. Instead, I log onto Twitter and find the tweet about Ms. McKay and delete it. I scan through the rest of messages. Maddie's been using the account for over a month. The tweets are random, mostly snarky comments about kids at school, but some are straight up nasty. This explains why some girl I never met slapped me in the face at a party two weeks ago. I delete everything and change the password to something Maddie will never figure out.

Jake clears his throat and says, "JT, don't forget to bring your phone up her as soon as you're done." I log out of Twitter and leave my phone face-down on Jake's desk. He nods and goes back to his *Sports Illustrated*.

I open a book and try to read, but it's no use. I'm too angry to concentrate. I'm angry with Maddie because she learned absolutely nothing after being suspended last fall and I'm mad at myself for covering for her. If I turn her in, she'll get expelled and won't be able to graduate. If I turn her in, I'll be committing social suicide. It's not that I wasn't anybody before I started dating Maddie, it's just that dating Maddie has made me more of a somebody.

Jake escorts me to the cafeteria at 12:15. I try not to make eye contact with anybody because I'm too mortified to explain why I'm not in class. Maddie slips behind me in the pizza line, cutting off a half dozen underclassmen. They complain, but she shuts them down with a menacing glare. She takes my arm and loud-whispers to me, "What's going on? Why haven't you answered any of my texts?"

"Because they won't let you use your phone in ISS. You should know that."

"Why are you in ISS?"

"Because somebody posted a nasty tweet about Ms. McKay on my account and she read it."

Her eyes get big and her eyebrows disappear into her bangs. "Oops."

"What do you mean 'Oops?' Why were you using my account? You're not even supposed to be on Twitter."

She rolls her eyes, "I'm not supposed to use my old account. Nobody said I can't open other ones."

"Other ones? How many do you have?"

"A few. I must have had yours open and used it by mistake." She digs her fingers dig into my arm. "You didn't tell anybody it was me, did you?"

"No, not yet. Ms. Deon said McKay was so upset she had to go home."

I pry her fingers off my arm but she clamps on again. "What do you mean *not yet*? You can't tell anybody. I'll get expelled if Ms. D finds out."

"I know that, but now I have five days in ISS because of you and I'm going to miss a track meet. Coach is going to kill me. I'm totally screwed because you dropped another stupid message bomb."

"Look, JT. This is your first offense. It doesn't even go on your record. Just do the suspension for me. I'll make it up to you. I'll do anything." She leans in close, brown eyes wide. "I can't get expelled. If my dad finds out he won't buy me a new car for graduation. Please, JT? For me? Your girlfriend? Who loves you and everything?"

I see Jake waiting for me by the cafeteria door with a lunch tray in his hands.

Maddie tightens her grip again. I drag her along with me as I load my tray with food. "Don't be mad at me. I'd do the same thing for you if you asked me to."

"Why would I have to ask you? I don't tweet horrible messages about people. By the way, I deleted all your tweets and changed the password."

"Why would you do that?"

"Seriously? Do you really need to ask?"

Maddie puts her chin on my shoulder and whispers in my ear. "Please, I'll make it up to you, just promise you won't say anything."

I ignore her and swipe my card for the lunch lady. This isn't one Maddie's usual screw-ups like promising me a ride to school, then forgetting to pick me up or blowing off our plans because her best buddy Trish found some stellar sale at the mall that they *had to* go to.

"Meet me at your car after school and I'll think about it." I slip out of her iron clutches and catch up with Jake, my Room 114 nanny.

Just after the fifth period bell rings, when I'm supposed to be in AP Calculus with Ms. McKay, who went home crying and probably hates my guts, Mr. Serrano, the head of the math department, shows up. One look at his face and I can tell he's not here because he baked a batch of cookies for me. He asks Jake if he can have a moment alone with me and Jake leaves for a bathroom break. I'm not sure he's supposed to do that; leave me alone with a teacher, not the bathroom thing.

Mr. Serrano pulls up a chair and straddles it with his arms resting on the back, like guys do in movies when they want to have a serious talk with the kid who has completely screwed up. It doesn't look comfortable to me, but there must be a reason they do it. Maybe because the last thing a kid wants to do is stare at someone's crotch, so they're forced to listen to what the teacher has to say.

Mr. Serrano takes a deep breath and shakes his head like I'm beyond hope. "JT, I find myself in a very difficult position. Ms. McKay showed me what you wrote about her. To say I'm disappointed is an understatement."

"Um, I can explain. It's, uh, sort of complicated."

"You've always been one of my top math students, a role model, someone that I could rely on to represent the Luther Burbank math department's commitment to excellence."

Mr. Serrano always brags about how well the school does on the state tests and in math competitions. To be specific, he brags about how well *I* do in the math competitions. It's not like I'm a genius or anything, I'm just good at math. Really good. It's dorky, but I won a couple of medals in the Math Olympics, which is a complete joke because I do track and field and there is nothing Olympian about a math competition. The only good thing about being so math-tastic is that I make decent money tutoring, which is way better than bagging groceries at the supermarket.

I have to think before I answer him. I could still rat Maddie out, but she'd never forgive me if I let her get expelled and she had to miss all the graduation parties. Ms. Deon said the suspension won't go on my record and Stanford or the scholarship committees will never find out, so it's really like a week of supervised study. I take a deep breath. Maddie better appreciate what I'm doing for her.

"I'm really sorry, Mr. Serrano. I'll apologize to Ms. McKay or whatever it takes to make it up to you guys."

"It's not that easy, JT. First of all, I'm going to have to remove you from Ms. McKay's class. She's not comfortable having you as a student anymore."

"But it's the only AP Calculus class."

"I'm well aware of that. I spoke to Ms. Deon and lucky for you, she overruled my decision to fail you for the quarter. You can do the assignments in the library and I'll grade your tests and quizzes."

I'm too shocked to say anything. He was going to fail me over a stupid tweet? This has nothing to do with my classwork. I haven't gotten one test question wrong all semester.

Mr. Serrano frowns at me, taking his glasses off to clean them on his shirt. "I may just be the 'moron that hired her,' but Ms. McKay is a teacher and while you may not agree with her methods, she deserves your respect. That's the problem with you kids. Respect. You have no respect for yourselves, for each other, or for adults. You write your little messages and don't think about how they affect people. It's all forgotten and you're on to the next thing." His voice gets louder and little spit bubbles foam in the corners of his mouth. This is getting a little scary and slightly gross. "Well, Mr. Monahan, I think it's time you learned that there are consequences for everything that you do." I sneak a peek at the door. Where the hell is Jake?

Mr. Serrano stands and leans on my desk, his face way too close, flecks of spit foam landing on my history book as he talks. "When you came to me for your college recommendations, I agreed to write them because I thought you were a decent, upstanding young man. However, your lack of respect for me and my department has given me serious doubts about your character." He steps away, puts his arms behind his back and paces in a circle around my desk, making me swivel my head like an owl to keep track of him. "I put my reputation on the line with each and every sentence that I write and if I can't stand behind the students that I recommend, then I lose my integrity. I think you should know that I'm seriously considering writing to the colleges that accepted you and to the scholarship committees that you applied to."

Wait. What? Can he even do that? I turn to face him.

"I already returned all the paperwork for Stanford. I *have to* go to college. I can't stay in Appleton the rest of my life," I blurt.

"Perhaps you should have thought of that before you insulted one of my teachers."

"Mr. Serrano, you know I'm a good student. I made a mistake," I struggle to come up with the right words to fix this. "Sometimes kids need to vent. It will never happen again."

Silence, except for the annoying lights, which sound like the buzzer they press when you get the answer wrong on a quiz show. I'm his favorite student, his mathematical wunderkind. He can't be doing this to me. I try to look repentant, but really, I'm pissed that Maddie can't control her stupid thumbs.

"I'm really sorry that Ms. McKay's feelings were hurt. There's got to be something that I can do to make it up to her *and* to you."

"This is a serious transgression, JT. I'm not sure how you can possibly make it up to either of us."

"Come on, Mr. Serrano. This is my whole life you're talking about. Ms. Deon is already punishing me with a week of suspension. Isn't writing to the colleges like, above and beyond?"

He stops pacing and stands over me, squinting and scrunching up his eyebrows. "This is my *word* on the line, JT. I've recommended a student that has not acted honorably. I'm not sure that I can live with that."

I plead, I grovel, I lose all sense of dignity. Is he really going to ruin my life over a stupid tweet? "Give me a chance to make it up to you."

Mr. Serrano shakes his head and walks to the door. I feel like I've just been handed a sentence to a life of go-nowhere jobs and living at home with my mom and grandmother. He stops and says, "I'll have to give it some more thought this weekend. I'll let you know my decision on Monday."

He walks out and I bury my face in my hands. I am so screwed.

Jake returns a couple of minutes after Mr. Serrano leaves. He gives me a guilty look. "Everything go OK?"

"Yeah, wonderful." Next time, don't abandon me, bathroom boy.

TWO
FRIDAY AFTERNOON

AFTER GETTING CHEWED out by Coach for being suspended, I grab some books from my locker and sprint outside to catch up with Maddie. She's leaning against her car, arms crossed, like she has more important things to do on a Friday afternoon than wait for me. Like most kids, she drives one of her parent's hand-me-down cars, but unlike most kids, her car is pretty sweet: it's a Volvo SUV with a million miles on it from all the weekend ski trips they take in the winter, but it's loaded and it has a turbo and she doesn't have to pay for gas or insurance.

I get a hug and a kiss with way too much tongue. Most days I'd go along with it and maybe go back to her house to fool around, but not today. I pull back. "That's not going to work."

She pouts and says, "What do you mean? I was just trying to show you how much I appreciate you sticking up for me."

"Maddie, I didn't stick up for you; I took the blame. There's a big difference."

"What do you mean?"

"I'm getting punished to save your ass. Now I've got Serrano all over my back. He's threatening to write to Stanford and the scholarship committees. I could be totally screwed."

"Well, if I get caught, I won't even be able to graduate. That's *so* much worse."

"Worse?! My whole college career could be down the toilet because of your stupid tweet. When are you going to learn to not shoot your mouth off online?"

"I don't know why you're being so mean to me. I said I would make it up to you." She wraps her arms around my waist and looks up at me. She smells like clean and lemon and mint and my mind starts to fuzz over. She smiles and says, "Let's go to my house. We can chill until my folks get home, then go to that party down at the sand pits. Trish says they're going to have kegs."

I shake my head and remind myself I'm still mad at her. "I can't. You know I have to go home and make dinner for my grandmother."

"Yeah, but you're usually at track practice now, so we have like two whole hours. We can get your grandma a pizza and drop it off."

I pull Maddie's hands off my waist and walk around to the other side of the car. My hormone levels return to normal and my brain fog clears. "She's not supposed to eat pizza. Her cholesterol is through the roof. Just give me a ride home and we can go to the party later."

We don't say much on the drive. She's bummed out because I'm mad at her, but what does she expect? Not only do I have to keep her little secret if I don't want her to get kicked out of school, now I have Serrano on my case and I have to find some way to convince him that I'm not a complete degenerate.

We pull into my driveway and sit in silence for a second. I hate fighting with Maddie, but it seems like we're arguing more and more lately. "You know I'm not going to tell Ms. D, right? I just wish you'd think twice before you go and badmouth somebody." I'm not forgiving her yet, but I'm trying to keep the peace. "You picking me up for the party?"

"OK, but I'm giving Trish a ride so we won't be able to do anything until later." Translation: we can mess around in the TV room in her basement after her mom and dad go to bed. I see her lean towards me for a good-bye kiss, but I pretend not to notice and open the door. It's petty, but she needs to know I'm not ready to move on.

I walk around the car and she rolls the window down. "What, no good-bye kiss?" I lean in, but she stops and glares at something over my shoulder. Helen Hernandez, my next-door neighbor and Luther Burbank Regional High School's rebel with way too many causes has just pulled into her driveway. Helen gets out of her van and spots us, walking over with her trademark smirk on her lips and a long silk scarf covering her recently-shaved head. If Maddie had hair on her back it would be standing straight up.

Helen and Maddie have been feuding since last spring when Helen accused Maddie of posting topless photos of her on some website. Nobody could ever prove that Maddie did it, but the whole school saw the photos before they got taken down. It was pretty embarrassing. Helen is pretty small on top and the caption read, "Worst case of mosquito bites ever." Kids still call her Mosquito Bites behind her back.

Maddie's eyes get squinty and her lips go thin and tight. Helen ignores her and pulls a stack of papers out of her messenger bag. "I got your homework." She's in all my classes except PE.

"Um, thanks. You didn't have to do that." Her t-shirt reads, *Boobs, they need your support*. How did she get that one past Ms. Deon?

"Yeah, I know, but I did it anyway." She gives Maddie the stink-eye and heads back to her house.

Maddie yells after her, "Hey, Helen, you know they have special shampoo for lice. You didn't have to shave your head to get rid of them."

Helen doesn't even flinch. She just keeps walking as if she didn't hear anything. Maddie looks at me and says, "How can you live next to her? She's such a weirdo."

"I'll ask my mom to put the house up for sale this weekend."

"No, really, JT. The girl needs help. Who shaves their head and wears such hideous clothing? And what's with her obsession with boobs? You'd think somebody that flat-chested would avoid the topic."

"Her aunt has breast cancer; that's how she's dealing with it. Listen, I have to check on my grandmother. What time are you picking me up?"

"How about eight?" She glowers over my shoulder at Helen's house. "Don't tell loser about the party. We don't need her there with her stupid pink ribbons."

"I hardly ever talk to Helen. Why would I tell her about the party?" I give Maddie a kiss and watch her back out of the driveway, just missing a pack of middle school kids walking home.

I never know what I'll find when I get home from school. My mom leaves for work at 3:00 and the late bus usually drops me off around 5:30. That leaves two and a half hours for my grandmother to get herself into trouble. She's somewhere between early and middle stage Alzheimer's and every day with her is a new adventure. I check the living room first and find her sitting in front of the TV. I check the screen and a very nervous-sounding boy is doing play-by-play for a middle school softball game.

"Mamo, what the heck are you watching?"

She waves the remote at me. "I can't get this damn thing to work. I think it's broken."

"It's not broken, you just hit the wrong buttons again. Where's the cheat-sheet I made for you?" I see it peeking out from under her butt. I tell her to lean forward and pull on the paper, but it tears in half. Damn. I'll have to print another one.

"Mamo, what do you want to watch?"

"That lesbian girl is funny. Put her on."

"*Ellen* isn't on for another half hour. How about something else?" I scroll through the channel guide and find an *NCIS* rerun. Mark Harmon melts her butter. Mamo's words, not mine.

I go to my room and try not to think about my little crisis. I can't believe Serrano is busting my ass over this stupid tweet. It wasn't really about him, but he's taking it personally because he hired Ms. McKay and she's totally incompetent. Maddie thinks he's hooking up with her, but I doubt it's that. With him, it's all about image. Every year he goes nuts about how the school is ranked on the state math exams. He wants us to finish in the top percentiles so he looks good.

I open my laptop and look for Mamo's TV cheat-sheet. My computer is so out of date it's humiliating, but I can't afford anything new right now. I bump the type up a few more point sizes and print it along with a new copy of the microwave instructions because Mamo spilled coffee all over the old one this morning.

I do homework for a couple of hours then call it quits and start dinner. Mamo used to be a good cook before the Alzheimer's started messing with her memory. I took over when she scorched a pan and almost set the kitchen on fire. My mom is definitely not a cook. She's more likely to pick up the phone and order take-out than plan a meal. I guess I take after Mamo. I actually like cooking. It gives me time to figure my problems out.

I've spent all day thinking about Maddie's tweet, but no matter how much I try to change the topic in my brain, it keeps coming back. I can't believe she didn't learn anything from last fall. Maddie got all bent out of shape because Jackie Thompson beat her out as captain of the field hockey team and Maddie posted some really nasty comments about her on Twitter and Facebook.

Jackie took them to Ms. Deon and after some major damage control by Maddie's parents, she was lucky to get away with a week of ISS and an apology in front of the whole team. She also had to shut down her Facebook and Twitter accounts to prevent more cyber-bullying.

I fill two plates with steamed green beans and *cacio e pepe*, a pasta dish with cheese and pepper that I learned about from watching cooking shows with Mamo. I hand her a plate and join her on the couch. She takes a bite of the pasta and says, "I like the orange stuff. This needs more cheese." She tries to hide her smile as she fills her mouth with another forkful.

I take the remote and change the channel to Mamo's favorite game show. "I slave in the kitchen for you and this is the thanks I get?"

She picks up a green bean and pops it in her mouth before she gives me a cheesy kiss on the cheek. "Well, if this is the best you can do, I suppose I'll have to eat it."

I roll my eyes and twirl some pasta on my fork. "It's just one of the crosses you have to bear, Mamo."

THREE
STILL FRIDAY

SAND PIT PARTIES are pretty much what you think they are: a bunch of kids standing around in the dark in what used to be a huge glacial deposit of sand and gravel, but is now an abandoned depression in the ground at the end of a rutted dirt road, complete with a couple of rusted-out trucks, some collapsing shacks, and a NO TRESPASSING sign full of bullet holes from years of target practice. On a good night, somebody has the foresight to buy a keg or two of beer. For five bucks you get a big, red plastic cup and as much foamy beer as you can drink before the tap runs dry.

Occasionally, the cops show up and confiscate the beer and send everyone home, but they don't arrest anybody who isn't completely drunk or acting like an idiot. Most of the local cops spent their weekend nights here when they were in high school, so they can relate.

It's cold for mid-May, but the stars are out along with a bright half-moon, so you can spot a rock or stump before you trip over it. Most of the girls didn't dress warm enough and half the guys are standing around in shorts, looking cool clearly taking priority over basic survival skills. Maddie and Trish are included in that group. Both of them are shivering fifteen minutes after we get there. I give Maddie my hoodie and Trish convinces my friend Miles to lend her his fleece and we both pretend we're not cold while they look cute in our too-big jackets.

Miles and Trish have been flirting since she broke up with her boyfriend two weeks ago, but I think Trish is waiting for Maddie to give Miles her official seal of approval before she makes a move. Trish's last boyfriend was a total ass, so hanging out with them was painful at best. I think Miles will get the thumbs up from Maddie. He's a nice guy, maybe too nice for Trish.

Like Maddie, Trish can be vain, but she's pretty and has a nice body, so you weigh the good with the bad. I certainly do. It's not that Maddie is always horrible. She's really sweet and generous when she wants to be, which is most of the time with me. But if she lets her dark side out like she does with Helen, then run for cover.

Miles and Trish wander off together for refills, leaving me and Maddie alone for the first time tonight. She lets out a loud sigh and says, "Are we done fighting?"

"Yeah, but you get why I was mad, right?"

"Um, I'm a terrible person and you're not and I owe you for the rest of your life."

I don't want to spend the night arguing, so I force myself to count to ten before I say anything. "No Maddie, that's not even close. I'm in trouble because you used my account to insult two teachers and now one of them is threatening to ruin my life. What if Stanford takes my offer back and I lose my scholarships?"

She rolls her eyes. "That's not going to happen. Serrano is just saying that to scare you. I'm sure he'll forget about it by Monday."

"What if he doesn't?"

"Then tell him to get over it. It's just a random tweet."

"Yeah, that's going to work. I'm glad we had this talk."

"JT, schools don't really care about this stuff like they used to. It's not like you said some totally racist shit or said you wanted to murder someone."

I throw my hands up in the air. "I didn't say anything. That was you!"

Another eye roll. "Yeah, but Serrano thinks it was you, so my point is, it's not that big a deal."

Maddie's logic is making my brain hurt, so luckily, she changes the subject. She looks over to the line by the keg and says, "So, what do you think of Miles and Trish? Should we let them hook up?"

I shake my head. "Don't involve me in this. Miles is my friend. I'm not telling him who he can or can't be with. If they like each other, then let it happen."

She rolls her eyes at me. "I'm not living through another Darren with her. That guy was such a dick. I don't know what she saw in him."

"Well, Miles is a nice guy, so they'll be fine."

"But, can you tell him not to talk about *The Mandalorian* or those lame Marvel people? It's like talking to my little brother, only worse, because he's not ten years old."

"I'm pretty sure Miles only brings up that superhero stuff to stop you and Trish from yapping about your reality shows. Trust me, it gets a little boring."

I get the raised eyebrow treatment. "Excuse me. My shows are culturally relevant. *Captain America* is boring." My turn to roll my eyes. I can't believe I'm having this conversation. Maddie says. "So, you'll talk to Miles? If they start dating, we can hang out with them and I won't want to strangle him after an hour?"

"Yes, whatever." I see that Miles isn't waiting around for Maddie's seal of approval anyway. He keeps touching Trish's arm while he's talking to her and she's doing her hair twisting thing and looking at him sideways. Classic flirting moves. They'll be making out before the night is over.

An hour or so later, Maddie and Trish are gone for a pee break and an extended discussion about Miles, who is in line hoping for one more cup of beer. I'm not feeling particularly social, so I find a boulder to lean against while I contemplate how to deal with Ms. McKay and Mr. Serrano on Monday morning. Out of the corner of my eye, I see someone heading my way. Someone small and dressed like a longshoreman: jeans, boots, a navy deck jacket with the collar flipped up and a dark watch cap. When he gets closer, I realize it's not a guy, but Helen. What's she expecting, a blizzard? It's cold out, but it's not January.

She stops a few feet away from me and says, "John Taylor, I thought that was you." She knows I hate my real name, but she likes to use it anyway.

"Hey sailor, how long you on shore leave for?"

"Nice. At least I'm not freezing my ass off. Where's *your* coat?"

"I gave it to Maddie. She dressed to impress rather than for the weather report."

She nods and says, "Chivalry isn't dead, huh? Too bad vanity isn't either." She sits next to me. There's barely enough room for my butt on the rock, so I have to scooch over to share with her. "I forgot to tell you that we have a test coming up in world history next Friday. Everything we've covered since midterms will be on it."

I feel a little weird with her leaning against me. Before the topless photo mess with Maddie, Helen and I were friends. Now we hardly say more than an awkward hello to each other. She takes the cup from my hand and looks into it for a long second before she takes a sip without asking. She makes a frowny face and hands it back.

"Help yourself why don't you?"

"I just wanted to see if it was worth paying five bucks for. I'm going to say no."

"The keg's almost dry anyway. What are you doing here? You're not exactly a party girl."

"I'm here with Jimmy Driscoll. My parents think I need to get out more and socialize with my peers. I'm not sure I agree."

I laugh. Jimmy Driscoll is only one of the biggest jocks in the school, literally. He's a year behind us, and like his dad and older brothers, he's a physical specimen: tall and muscular and a natural at any sport he plays. Jimmy's on three varsity teams and will probably be captain for all of them next year like his brothers were.

"Please tell me you're not hooking up with Jimmy."

"God, no. That would be like kissing you." Helen's mom and Jimmy's mom have been best buds forever, so he practically grew up with the two of us. "Jimmy and his baseball bros tell me this is where Luther Burbank's social elite come to mingle. I have to say, I don't think I've been missing anything."

I shrug my shoulders. "I don't know, flat beer, a desolate landscape, the occasional drunk kid puking behind a pine tree; they say these are the best years of our lives."

Helen laughs. "You make it all sound so inviting. Since

you're the worldly-wise party-boy, maybe you have some advice on how to make this not suck."

I shoot her a sideways glance. "My advice is bring your own booze and drink in moderation and these things usually aren't that bad. If you're going to get hammered, make sure you have a friend who's watching out for you. That way, you can at least spend the night in a warm bed instead of lying in a pool of vomit."

"So, if I'm going to get shit-faced, bring a wing-man. I guess that's the rub, huh? Other than Jimmy and you, I don't really know anybody here."

"That's because you're such a freak." I look up as Maddie and Trish appear from behind an abandoned dump truck and stand, glowering at Helen. Why can't they just play nice for a change?

Helen smiles. "Madison, Patricia, you're out from under your bridge. What'd you do, run out billy goats to snack on?" Before they can break out into a verbal knife fight, another shape materializes from the dark. It's not a troll, but it's very large and moves like a stalking grizzly bear.

Jimmy gives me a nod and says, "JT, I hear you're doing time."

I shrug my shoulders. "Yeah, Ms. D has me in solitary. I hear you guys made the play-offs. Impressive."

"Bet your ass. Next stop, state champs, we're going all the way." Jimmy turns to Helen and says, "We're gonna blow this clambake and get some Chinese food. You coming or what?"

Maddie looks back and forth between Helen and Jimmy with her mouth hanging open. I can't help but laugh at her. Helen stands and says, "Fine, but I'm not splitting the bill. Last time you guys ordered everything on the menu. And tell Sully I got shotgun this time. I'm not sitting in back with Jonesy and

Snapper again. Those two argue like an old married couple." She waves goodbye to me, ignores Maddie and Trish, and has to run to keep up with Jim as he giant-steps over to where his truck is parked.

I push Maddie's chin up, closing her mouth, then do the same for Trish. Maddie stares at me and says, "What were you doing talking to that weirdo and since when does she hang out with Jimmy Driscoll?"

Her world order is in turmoil and I can't help but laugh again.

"It's not funny, JT. You know I can't stand that loser. If you're going to start hanging out with her, then you're walking home."

"Chill out, Maddie. She just came over to tell me about a history test. Speaking of home, I'm freezing. We should get going."

Trish says, "I want to say goodbye to Miles. Have you seen him?"

We go on a hunt for Miles and find him chatting up a bunch of track kids. Trish points her boobs at him and does some more hair flips and we end up in separate cars for a burger run before McDonalds closes.

Maddie drops me off around midnight. Mamo is asleep on the couch, so I wake her up enough to get her aimed towards her bedroom. I give her ten minutes to get changed then knock on her door. No answer, so I peek in.

She's got her pants bunched around her ankles and she's flopped back her bed, snoring. I hate when this happens. I take her shoes and socks off and drape her pants over a chair. I'm not brave enough to undress the rest of her, so I swing her legs onto the bed and cover her with a blanket. If my mom wants Mamo in her pajamas, she can deal with that when she gets home.

FOUR
SATURDAY MORNING

BARTENDER HOURS AREN'T EXACTLY family-friendly. I really only get to see my mother on weekends and after school on Monday and Tuesday. If she's up before noon on Saturday or Sunday, we get a few hours of quality time to nag each other about whatever has to be done around the house.

Today, my mother is in my doorway bright and early at 10:30 in her black silk robe with the Chinese dragon on the back and her hair in a towel. I've been up and dressed for a while, but I was hoping for at least another hour before I have to deal with any chores. She bends over to wrap the towel tighter around her hair and then straightens up gives me a tired look. She must have had a long night at the bar. I didn't hear her get home until almost 3 AM.

Compared to my friends' mothers, she's young, but then my friends' mothers didn't get pregnant at nineteen. She's also pretty fit even though she doesn't do anything to keep herself in shape. She claims working a busy bar all night is all the exercise she needs. I guess it works because she buys her jeans at the same store as Maddie and Trish instead of at the Foxy Lady where all the other mothers shop.

"JT, what's this I hear from your principal about a Twitter message?"

"It's nothing, Ma."

"Don't tell me it's nothing. Getting a phone call from your principal is not nothing. Why would you post that horrible message anyway?"

"It wasn't me. Somebody used my account."

"Then why are you being punished? Didn't you tell Ms. Deon?"

"Not really; it's complicated. I can't tell her who did it because they would get in worse trouble."

"JT, you got suspended. What can possibly be worse than that?"

"It's only in-school suspension. It's like solitary confinement. Besides, it doesn't go on my record, so it's no big deal."

She folds her arms across her chest and glares at me. "No, it is a big deal, bucko, because I'm going to make it one. Tell me who wrote the message. I didn't raise you to be a patsy for some dumb-ass kid who goes around insulting teachers."

"It wasn't some dumb-ass kid."

She squints at me, one eyebrow cocked. "Please tell me it wasn't Maddie." I don't say anything, so she rolls her eyes and swears under her breath. "You have got to be kidding me. Did she not learn anything from that mess she got herself into last fall?"

"I didn't say it was Maddie."

"You didn't have to, JT. I could see it on your face. Well, if you're dumb enough to cover for that girl, then you can take the punishment. And for being dumb enough to take somebody else's punishment, I'm going to add to your misery. You're grounded."

I throw my hands up in the air. "That's ridiculous. You can't ground me. You've never grounded me."

"Well, you've never been this stupid before. No parties, no hanging out with Maddie, no nothing for a month. You come home after school and spend a nice quiet evening with your grandmother."

I flop onto my desk chair. "Give me a break, Ma. Maddie and I have tickets to a concert next Saturday. You can't do this."

"I can and I am. That's as long as you don't do anything else stupid between now and then and make it worse."

"But Ma, I'm graduating in three weeks. I'll miss all the parties."

"Then tell Ms. Deon that Maddie wrote the message. It's your choice. Stay stupid and you stay grounded. Smarten up and you're free to go." She unwraps her hair from the towel and runs her fingers through the dark red strands. She's 38 and still no signs of gray hair. Mamo has the same brown eyes and red hair and didn't go gray until she was in her fifties. I must have inherited my blue eyes and dark brown hair from my father, whoever he is, because I don't have a hint of red.

"Come on, Ma. What about the concert? How about if you ground me starting next week?"

"Sorry, JT, my decision is final. You can tell Maddie that she's the reason you're grounded. Besides, this whole mess could completely screw up your chances to get scholarships. You know we can't afford that fancy school in California if you don't get scholarships."

"Ma, Stanford gave me tons of money, all the other scholarships are just for expenses like beer and prostitutes." I get the squint. God, she's grouchy before eleven.

"Don't even try to joke your way out of this one, buddy boy. It's not going to work. I don't know what you see in that girl, anyway. She never comes in the house, just pulls up out front and beeps the horn. Who was she raised by, cab drivers?"

Not this again. "Ma, why would I invite her in? This place is embarrassing. We don't even have HBO or any streaming services. What would we possibly do, sit on the couch with Mamo and watch *Law and Order* re-runs all night?"

"You make it sound like that would be a punishment. Your grandmother could use some company." She starts to leave but stops in my doorway. "Don't forget about that leaky vent on the roof. We're supposed to get a big storm this week and you told me you could do it, so I didn't bother to call Mr. Hernandez."

"Ma, you don't get the neighbors to fix your roof for you. You hire somebody."

"Or you get your perfectly healthy son to do it. You said it was easy when you looked it up on the internet."

I'm not going to win this argument. "Fine. I'll fix the vent today. Now can I at least go to the concert next week? The tickets were expensive."

"What part of *no* don't you get, JT? Take the car and buy whatever you need to fix the roof. There's money in my wallet and bring back the change. Oh, and pick up some pee pads for your grandmother while you're out."

I let out a groan. "Maaa, not pee pads. Do you have any idea how embarrassing it is to buy those? There's always some girl at the register laughing at me."

"For God's sake, JT, she'll know they're not for you. And pick up a box of Senokot. The new pain meds they put Mamo on are making her constipated. The keys are in my purse." She flips the towel over her shoulder and walks down the hall to her room. Conversation over.

Wonderful. I get to risk my life on the roof *and* buy pee pads *and* laxatives *and* no Styrofoam Rockets concert next week. Not that I was dying to go see some boy band from New Jersey, but it was Maddie's birthday present. She is going to have a fit, but I'll just tell her what my options are. That will take some of the piss out of her. Still, I'm going to be out the money for the ticket. Maybe I can sell it to one of Maddie's friends.

What's even worse is I'm going to miss all the graduation parties, which will be a monumental suck-fest. Maybe I can get my mother to change her mind before then.

Yeah, and maybe Maddie will stop thinking about herself before anybody else.

FIVE
SATURDAY AFTERNOON

I GET BACK from my errands and make myself something to eat. Ma needs to buy more groceries, so there are only enough cold cuts for four sandwiches. Doesn't she get that I'm still growing? I'd complain, but she's still being a pill about the suspension. I go outside to eat my lunch in the front yard and stare at the leaky vent pipe. According to the guys at the hardware store and the video I watched on fixit.com, this shouldn't take that long. All I need is a ladder, which, of course, we don't have.

Our neighbors have ladders, but I have to think about which one I want to deal with today. Mr. Weeks, the old guy across the street, will talk my ear off for the rest of the afternoon and I'll feel guilty when I finally leave because he lives alone and his daughters live too far away to visit often. Mr. Hernandez has ladders, but I'd have to possibly deal with Helen and after yesterday, I've seen enough of her for a while. The new couple that just moved in down the street probably has a ladder, but I only wave hello when I drive by, I haven't actually talked to either of them.

The problem resolves itself when Helen comes out her side door with a bag of garbage in her hands. She nods at me and disappears into her garage. I finish the first sandwich and wait for her to come back out.

She sees me watching for her and gets her sarcastic smirk. "S'up, party-boy?"

"Is your dad home? I was hoping I could borrow a ladder."

"Nope. Just me. What do you need? We got step stools, step ladders, you name it."

"Do you still have that big one? I have to get up on my roof."

She nods. "No problemo. Come on over; don't be bashful." She eyes my lunch and says, "Are those all for you?"

"Yup."

"Seriously? I haven't had lunch yet. Can I have one?"

I hold the plate away from her which isn't hard because she's such a runt. "No way. I'm starving."

"You have to be kidding me. How many have you had already?"

"Just one. Get your own lunch."

"Fine. I just remembered that my dad lent the ladder to my Uncle Dante."

I point into the garage. "It's right there hanging on the wall."

"That's a different ladder. That one will cost you a sandwich if you want to borrow it." She raises her eyebrows, challenging me. Damn her. I knew I should have asked Mr. Weeks. At least he wouldn't try to scam my lunch off me. I hold out the plate and she plucks a sandwich from the top and opens it up to check it out.

"You used Dijon Mustard, right, not that yellow stuff?"

"Yes."

She lifts the lettuce up and pokes at the cheese. "What kind of cheese is this? It better not be American."

"It's Provolone. Can we stop with the questions and get the ladder already?"

She takes a bite and leans against her car. "Chill, JT. Let me eat my lunch first."

After she eats my sandwich and follows me inside so she can drink my last bottle of iced tea, Helen helps me carry the ladder and set it up against the front of my house. I'm torn between finding a polite way to get rid of her and letting her stay in case I fall off the roof and need somebody to tell my mother to call 911. She settles the debate by climbing up after me and walking along the roof ridge like it's a balance beam.

I forgot how fearless she is. My house is only a one-story ranch, but the roof is slippery with pine needles and moss and I take my time creeping over to the bathroom vent with my bag of tools and supplies. Helen perches on the ridge a few feet away from me and says, "You know what you're doing?"

"How hard can it be?"

Helen scoots closer and says, "I helped my dad do this on our house last summer. You have to seal it up properly or it's going to leak like crazy."

Half an hour later, I'm wiping caulk off my hands and shoving everything back in the plastic bag. Helen checks my work and says, "Not bad, JT. Almost looks professional. Should we do head butts or some other male bonding ritual to celebrate?" This gets a smile from me.

"Thanks for your help. That wasn't as easy as I thought it would be."

"Any time." She climbs back up to the roof ridge and says,

"Come check this out. Remember when we were little kids and we tried to bungee-jump from up here? The rope is still tied around the chimney."

I do a granny-walk over to where she's standing and look at the rotted clothesline then peek over the edge of the roof to the lawn that I have to mow tomorrow. I don't know how Helen talked me into that stunt. We tied bungee cords to the clothesline and Helen jumped first. Luckily, all she broke was her arm, but her mom and dad almost killed both of us *and* her older sister who was supposed to be watching us, instead of yakking on the phone in her bedroom.

I cut the old rope off the chimney and stuff it in the bag. "That was probably the stupidest idea we ever had, huh?"

She stares at me for a couple for seconds, clearly debating her response. "Stupidest idea *I* ever had. You have me beat since then." I know she's talking about Maddie. I think about apologizing for Maddie's comments yesterday, but it will probably just wind Helen up and I'm not in the mood for one of her lectures.

She sits on the roof ridge again and pats the shingles next to her, clearly not ready to climb down yet. "Talk to me, JT. What have you been up to lately?"

I shrug my shoulders and sit down. We can see down the road to the town athletic fields, where little kids are being screamed at by their parents in the age-old tradition of Little League baseball.

My mother comes out dressed for work and squints at us, her hand shading her eyes. Helen waves and says, "Hey, Ms. Monahan. How's it going?"

"Helen, is that you? What happened to all your hair?"

"I donated it to Locks of Love, then shaved my head to show my solidarity for my Auntie Lin. It'll grow back."

My mom frowns. I could never see her cutting her hair off for any cause. She's too addicted to the compliments she gets on it. "Well, that's nice of you. Tell Lin I've been thinking of her." She takes a step towards her car, but stops and says, "JT, remember what I told you. I'm going to call during my break, so you better answer the phone. And no visitors."

She gets in the car and it takes her a few tries to get it started. I keep telling her she has to pump the pedal twice *then* turn the key, but she never remembers. Helen waits until the car turns the corner before she says anything. "Your mom grounded you?"

I don't bother to look at her. "Yup. She's pissed about the whole Twitter thing."

"Well, yeah, why wouldn't she be? You're a total sucker for taking the blame for Maddie."

I look at her sideways. "Quiet, you. I don't need anybody else giving me grief. Besides, how do you even know Maddie did it?"

She kicks a clump of moss loose with the heel of her sneaker and picks it up to examine it. "Please, it's obvious she's been using your account. The tweets are classic Madison Beauchamp: full of typos and devoid of punctuation. You text like you're writing a term paper. I'm surprised you don't use footnotes and a bibliography." She stares at me. "What do you see in her? I'm serious, tell me what the attraction is."

I've been asking myself the same question, but I'm not going to admit it to Helen. When a pretty, popular girl pays attention to you, most guys don't stop and ask her to take a compatibility test. "She's got lots of good qualities, you just have to know her better."

She lip-farts in response. "What happened to you, JT? You

37

used to be a great guy. Now all you care about is being popular and parties and bone-head stuff like that."

"Nothing happened to me. I'm the same as I always was."

"No, you're the same on the outside, but different on the inside. You're like this hollow shell, totally lacking substance, like one of those crappy, fake chocolate bunnies you get in your Easter basket. What do you believe in? What makes you get out of bed in the morning?"

"My alarm clock."

She does a little snort-laugh. "Very funny. There's more to life than sitting at the cool table at lunch and drinking beer down at the sand pits. You have to look beyond yourself. Think about others. Change the world. If everybody did just one little thing to initiate change, it would make a difference."

I watch her for a few long seconds. "You really believe that stuff, don't you? You think your little five-foot-two bald self can change the world. I guess I admire the dedication, but what you're doing really isn't tangible. You're never going to see any results. Shaving your head or wearing a t-shirt isn't going to find a cure for cancer. It's all a waste of time if you ask me."

"That's where you're wrong. Every little bit matters. Maybe shaving my head won't cure cancer, but if the wig they make out of my hair helps a chemo patient feel good about herself then I've made a difference in one person's life. I can be happy with that. What have you done to help somebody else lately? Covering for Maddie's Twitter abuse doesn't count because that's just being an accessory after the fact."

We lock eyes for a couple of seconds before I turn away.

"Right now, I can only deal with making a difference in one person's life: mine. I didn't work my ass off to get into a good school so I could spend the rest of my life surrounded by apple orchards and falling down barns."

"So that's the plan, run away and leave us all behind?"

"Like you're going to miss this place." I don't wait for a response. "We should probably get back down. I have to check on Mamo."

She snort-laughs again. "Yeah, I got stuff to do, too."

I help Helen put the ladder away and thank her for helping me. I get the smirk. "Any time, hollow bunny boy. That's what friends are for, even if we're not really friends anymore." It's no wonder that I always feel guilty whenever I talk to Helen.

SIX
SATURDAY NIGHT

I PUT off my dreaded phone call to Maddie as long as I can. We don't really have any plans, but it's Saturday and doing something together is implied. Needless to say, she's not pleased.

"You didn't tell her it was me, did you?"

"No, she figured it out on her own."

"What does that mean?"

"It means she figured out that you posted the message. Anyway, she's pissed that I'm covering for you, so I'm grounded unless I rat you out to Ms. Deon."

Silence. All I hear is Maddie's breathing. She's got bad allergies, so she's a mouth breather. "You still there?"

"Yeah, but you're not going to do that, right?"

"No, Maddie, I told you I wouldn't. Anyway, I'm working on her. I should be able to wear her down by next Saturday."

"Oh my God! The Styrofoam Rockets! She has to let you go. It's my birthday present."

"I told you, I'm working on her. Maybe I'll get time off for good behavior."

"You know, this totally sucks. Trish has a stupid date with Miles tonight, so that means I have nothing to do."

"I'd feel sorry for you if this whole thing wasn't your fault to begin with."

"That's so not fair, JT. It was an accident. You need to stop bringing that up because we all have secrets. It would suck if your mom and Ms. Deon found out about some of yours."

"What are you talking about?"

"I'm sure certain teachers would love to know who stole a bunch of real estate signs and put their houses up for sale last month."

"You're not exactly innocent. You were the one driving."

"Yeah, but it was your idea. Trish and I said it was stupid, but you and Darren insisted."

"Yeah, well I already told you I wasn't going to tell anybody so you don't have to get nasty."

"I'm not being nasty, I'm just saying we all have secrets."

"Whatever. Call me later, OK? I'll be bouncing off the walls by nine o'clock."

Maddie doesn't call me. I don't know if she's pissed or found something else to do, but I text her a couple of times and get nothing. Fabulous. She probably let the battery on her phone run out again.

I go back into the living room to sit with Mamo. We're in the middle of a *Lord of the Rings* marathon and she's having trouble following the plot. She furrows her brows and says,

"Explain this to me again. Gandalf didn't die? He just fought that fire thing and turned white?"

"Yeah, sort of." Where is Miles when I need him? He knows this stuff cold. "He defeated the Balrog and achieved a higher state of being. White wizards are more powerful the gray wizards."

She contemplates this for a few seconds, shifting around in her seat to ease the pain in her back. "So, it's kind of like getting a promotion."

"Sure, why not?"

"OK, now explain those tree guys again."

It goes on like this until she starts to nod off around 11:00. I get her up and have her get ready for bed. Ma calls the landline just before midnight. She's a clever girl. If she called my cell phone, I could try to pull a fast one on her.

I can be clever, too. "Appleton State Prison, maximum security. How may I help you?"

"Very funny, JT. How's it going? Is Mamo in bed yet?"

"I just tucked her in. She said I was a nice boy and told me I reminded her of her grandson." Ma is silent on the other end. I say, "She can't remember who I am, but she can remember her chocolate."

She lets out a long sigh. "I think those new painkillers are making things worse. You took the chocolate away for the night, right?"

"Yeah, but she wasn't happy about it. She said someone told her she could have candy any time she wanted. She snuck a couple of pieces in her purse when she thought I wasn't looking, but I let her have them. Someday she's going to stumble onto your stash and we're going to find her in a chocolate coma."

Mamo is seriously addicted to chocolate. She goes through

a whole bag of dark chocolate squares a day. My mother buys it in bulk when she finds a sale and we dole it out a bag at a time. We have to take them from her before she goes to sleep or she'll eat chocolate in bed all night. The last time I took Mamo to the dentist, she had to have a tooth pulled because it was all black and rotten. Gruesome.

She also hides chocolates around the house like a squirrel hides nuts. The problem is, with her memory being so poor, she never remembers where she hid them. I find them under cushions, behind books on the shelves, even in the bathroom medicine cabinet. It's like Easter morning every day of the year.

I ponder bugging my mother about the concert next weekend, but drop it. Not while she's at work. I have all week to work on her. I say goodbye and put the phone back in the kitchen and shut the house down, leaving lights on for my mother when she gets home.

I get into bed and shut my lights off. I wonder what Maddie ended up doing without me. It's weird to not hear from her all night, not even a text. I'll have to give her crap her tomorrow for letting her phone die again. I roll over onto my side and stair out my window. I can see lights on at Helen's house. Her mom will be getting home late, too. Saturdays are always busy at the restaurant she owns.

I turn on the light near my bed and open up the drawer on my nightstand. I don't know why I suddenly remember it, but when we were little kids, before we got our own cell phones, Helen and I had Spiderman walkie-talkies so we could talk to each other. I root around in the drawer and find mine in the back, buried under everything.

I can't believe I still have it. I turn it on, but it doesn't work. I open up back and the batteries are all corroded, the insides leaking out and ruining the contacts. It will never work again, so I toss it in the trash. I wonder if Helen still has hers. Probably not. I wouldn't blame her if she never talked to me after what happened last year, but for some reason, she still does. I usually get a dose of abuse each time, but she still talks to me nonetheless.

Girls are a different kind of cruel than boys. Boys are cruel in a physical way: wedgies and swirlies at school, elbows and cheap shots on the basketball court, kicks when you're not looking in soccer. I'm not saying that girls can't throw an elbow when they want to, because I've seen some nasty things go down on the girls' soccer field. With girls though, it's more of a mental game: hurtful comments, hard looks and the age-old stand-by, pretending you don't exist.

Maddie's like that with Helen, but I don't understand why. They used to be friends in middle school. They weren't like best friends for life or anything, but they hung out together once in a while and I got to know Maddie a little. Both of them were skinny tomboys that were fun to shoot hoops with at the court down the street.

Things changed before freshman year. Puberty hit Maddie with a vengeance that summer and she got boobs and curves and grew a couple of inches. When we started high school in the fall, all the older boys noticed her and she clearly liked the attention. She started dating a junior and then she became like Luther Burbank royalty.

After that, Maddie and Helen didn't hang out much at all. Helen and I still did stuff together, but she would get pissed if I asked about Maddie because she figured out that I had a crush on her like every other boy in school. It's not like Helen and I would ever hook up or anything, so it wasn't that she was jealous. Helen said Maddie had gone over to the dark side and was thinking with her boobs. I didn't see how that was a problem.

Junior year, Helen got uber-political. I still hung out with her at home, but not so much at school, because she was becoming a major outcast. It's hard enough to survive high school without flying a freak flag over yourself every day. Besides, I was doing really well in sports and girls were noticing me. I was even getting looks from Maddie.

Let's face it, it's hard to flirt successfully when Helen shows up in the middle of a conversation and asks if you've heard about some obscure act of inhumanity that occurred in some remote African village or South American jungle. It's even worse when she's wearing eighty rubber bracelets from all her pet causes and dressed in some fashion nightmare from the Salvation Army reject pile.

I'm not exactly proud of it, but I chose popularity over Helen and stopped hanging out with her. I used sports and tutoring and anything else as an excuse when she asked me to do something and after a while, she stopped asking. When I started dating Maddie, she pretty much stopped talking to me altogether.

My life was practically Helen-free until somebody posted the photos. Somehow, they got shots of Helen in the shower after swimming at the YMCA pool, eyes closed, washing her hair, but head-on, boobs in plain view.

Helen accused Maddie and Trish and I had to take a side. Maddie told me she didn't do it and I believed her. Helen called me an idiot and we had a major blow-up and she said that she was done with me. I didn't lose too much sleep over it. In fact, the fight with Helen was pretty much a relief. I didn't have to feel guilty about ignoring her anymore. Well, not *as* guilty.

SEVEN

SUNDAY

MY ONLINE SEARCH for new shoes is interrupted by my mother and grandmother arguing in the bathroom. I hear my name mentioned more than once so I try to block it out. Whatever they're fighting about, dragging me into it can't be good. Besides, it's no way near as important as finding a new pair of crossword puzzle Vans. My old ones are beat to crap and all I can find online in my size is the pink version, which are clearly girl shoes. I may have to settle for the standard Jeff Spicoli black and white check. Lame.

The bathroom ruckus settles down and five minutes later my mother is looking over my shoulder with her hands on her hips, red-faced and frowning. Time to pretend I have tons of homework.

I spin my chair to face her. "Hello, Mother. How are you this fine morning?"

"I'm not in the mood JT. Mamo woke up soaked again. She's going to have to start wearing Depends at night. I'm going to need you to make sure she puts them on if I'm not here."

"Ma, NO. Please."

"JT, she's not going to remember by herself and I'm sick to death of washing her sheets and pajamas every other day."

"But she's my grandmother. I'm not supposed to know anything about her underwear problems. This is crossing some line into child abuse. I may need to call the authorities."

"JT. Enough. I need your help. I can't do this by myself. It's not like I ask a lot from you."

I skip the eye roll because it pisses her off to no end. "No, just cooking, cleaning, shopping, mowing the lawn, taking out the trash. I live a life of leisure."

She crosses her arms and glares down at me. "And I pay for everything."

"No, you don't. I pay for my own clothes with my tutoring money. I don't even ask you for an allowance anymore, not that you ever remembered to give it to me."

She squints her eyes and huffs her breath in frustration. "I'm not going to argue about this. Make sure Mamo is wearing Depends before she goes to bed. I'll put a box under the sink along with her pee pads."

I glare back at her. "Fine. When I'm psychologically damaged and can't have normal relationships, I'll tell my psychiatrist all about this."

She sits down on the edge of my bed and buries her face in her hands. She doesn't say anything for a while, just sniffs a lot, so I'm pretty sure she's crying. My mother never cries. She's too much of a hard-ass. I think about putting my arm around her shoulder, but we're just not a huggy family. I'd probably surprise her and get an elbow in the ribs.

I roll my chair over to her and lean down, trying to catch her eye. "Ma, look, I'm sorry. I'll help Mamo. I'm already damaged so it's not like it will make things any worse." She looks up at me and snuffles her nose with the back of her hand. Her eyes are red and her lashes are all damp. Definitely crying.

I say, "Yesterday she stuck a pee pad on the outside of her pants. What happens when we can't leave her alone?"

"We'll deal with it. We're her family and I promised her I'd never put her in a nursing home."

"But someday you may have to. I'm not always going to be here to help. What are you going to do in September?"

She doesn't look at me. "She's fine, JT. It's just the new medication. The doctor said the confusion will go away after a couple of weeks."

"What if it doesn't? What if her Alzheimer's is getting worse?"

She stands up and folds her arms across her chest. She still won't look at me. "It's the medicine. She'll be fine." I don't argue with her. My mother is blind when it comes to Mamo. It's like if she doesn't admit something, then it won't happen.

I get a stack of cookies from the kitchen and stick my head in the living room to check on my grandmother. She's all slumped down and sad looking, so I plunk myself on the couch next to her. I figure she needs some company after her fight with my mother. I offer her a cookie, but she shakes her head. It's oatmeal raisin, probably too healthy for her.

"Mamo! S'up? How's the world treating you today?"

"Your mother's in a bad mood today. I'd steer clear of her if I were you."

"Too late. She already found me." I pick up the remote and turn on the TV. "Anything good on today? What you in the mood for?"

She shrugs and looks totally bummed out, so I elbow her. "How about some Discovery Channel? I saw an ad for a show where they drop you off in the middle of nowhere naked. I think you're supposed to find food and shelter and stuff. Sounds pretty weird."

She looks at me sideways and says, "Who would sign up for that?"

"I don't know. Nude survivalists? I'd bet you'd watch it if Mark Harmon was on the show, you know, like naked NCIS."

She turns and looks at me full on. "Where would he put his gun?"

"I don't know, in a strategically place holster?"

"That's just a stupid idea. Why would they make the characters naked? How can you solve crimes if you don't have any clothes? They're just going to ruin the show. Why do those idiots in Hollywood always ruin perfectly good shows?"

"Jeez, Mamo, don't get so literal on me. They're not going to change the show. I was just making a joke."

"Well, it's not funny. I don't appreciate you making fun of me either."

I lean into her. "I'm not making fun of you Mamo. I'm trying to cheer you up. You want to play some cards or Scrabble?" We're supposed to play games with her to keep her mind sharp, but lately she doesn't like playing because she gets confused.

"No, JT, I just want to sit here. By myself if it's not too much trouble." This isn't good. When she gets depressed, she starts crying and my mother gets frustrated because she doesn't know how to handle it. I pick up the Sunday paper and find the crossword puzzle and start filling it in. Mamo used to be a crossword genius, doing them in pen. I use a pencil.

"What's a six-letter word for jungle cat?"

"Jaguar." I do a couple of more by myself.

"What's a falcon-headed Egyptian god, five letters?"

"Horus."

I elbow her. "You making that up? How do you spell it?"

She elbows me back. "H-O-R-U-S. What's the next one?" She leans over me to read the clues. "Five down is *asp*." I fill in the boxes and take a bite out of a cookie. Mamo starts rattling off answers one after another. Mission accomplished.

EIGHT
EARLY MONDAY

THERE'S nothing worse than having to apologize when you don't mean it, except maybe when you have to apologize for something you didn't do. I spent Sunday afternoon mowing the weeds in my yard, doing homework, and trying to come up a decent apology for Ms. McKay. No matter how much I thought about it, I couldn't get it to sound right in my head.

Maddie wasn't any help because she had to go to her uncle's house for the day with her mom and dad and was totally unavailable. We texted back and forth a couple of times. First, she told me she couldn't talk because she was with her family, then she had too much homework. Since when is she so dedicated to her classes?

So now it's Monday morning and I'm still struggling with what I'm going to say to Ms. McKay. I'm so spaced out I don't see Helen backing out of her driveway and I walk right into her path.

She hits the brakes and leans out the window. "Wake up,

JT, I almost killed you." My heart is racing because my flight response has kicked in five seconds too late to do anything for me, so I just wave and step out of her way. She backs her car out onto the street and pulls up even with me. "You want a ride?"

I shake my head. "No, I'm good, thanks." She shrugs her shoulders and takes off for school. I walk down the street and wait for the bus with a couple of gawky freshmen boys and a sophomore girl. I'm the only senior on the bus because most kids either have a car or get a ride from somebody that does. If Maddie didn't drive all the way out to Trish's house on the other side of town, she could pick me up in the morning, but I gave up on that dream long ago. I talk to the girl sometimes because she runs track, but mostly I stand off by myself and wish I had a car.

Ms. Deon shows up in ISS right after the first period bell with another kid for Jake to keep an eye on. I've seen him around. Everybody calls him Wolverine because he's short and muscled up and has long hair and sideburns. He used to be a good wrestler, but he got kicked off the team for biting a kid during a match. The rumor mill says he bit a finger off, but I have friends who wrestle and they say he bit him on the leg and didn't even draw blood. Either way, he's not somebody you want to back into a corner or poke with a stick.

Wolverine picks a chair a couple of rows away from me and Ms. Deon asks me, "You ready? Ms. McKay and Mr. Serrano are meeting us in my office in ten minutes."

I'm not, but I say I am. The halls are empty and quiet

except for the clacking of her heels and the squeak of my sneakers on the floors. Ms. Deon tries to make small talk by asking me about my weekend, but I'm not really into it so I keep my answers simple. We get to her office and I take a seat at her table, facing the door. I don't want anybody sneaking up behind me.

I truly don't know what I'm going to say until Ms. McKay walks into the room with Mr. Serrano. Like her attempts to be a cool teacher, Ms. McKay's humiliation is painfully obvious. She doesn't look at me, but nods to Ms. Deon and takes a seat and stares out the window. Mr. Serrano glares at me like I'm some kind of bug, but I ignore him and put words together in my head.

Ms. Deon says, "Well, first of all, thank you for coming down. I'd like to keep this meeting brief and to the point." She turns to me and nods. "JT, I believe you have something to say."

I want Maddie to be here. I want her to see how words can hurt somebody. Yes, Ms. McKay is a suck-tastic teacher, but that doesn't mean you should rub her nose in it in front of the whole world.

I keep it short and to the point, but something tells me my apology isn't going to do much to fix what's wrong here. "I'm very sorry, Ms. McKay. The message was irresponsible and immature. Nobody deserves to be publicly humiliated like that. I know this will probably sound hollow at this point, but if there is anything that can be done to make it up to you, please let me know."

Ms. McKay looks at me briefly. She folds her hands on the table and says, "There isn't anything. I just want to move on."

Just stamp "Beyond Redemption" on my forehead.

She turns to Mr. Serrano, who stares at me for a few

seconds then clears his throat. "JT, I put a lot of thought into this matter over the weekend and although I have not made a final decision, I'm still strongly leaning towards writing a letter to the colleges that accepted you and the scholarship committees that you applied to. I put my reputation on the line when I recommended you and I don't see any other way around this."

Ms. Deon frowns at him and says, "Why is this the first time I've heard about this? The rules clearly state that this matter is to be handled by a five-day suspension and that it is not to be entered into the student's record. There's no need to punish JT further. He's offered what I believe is a sincere apology and he will serve the rest of his suspension and the matter will be closed. We've already made arrangements for him to finish what's left of AP Calculus in supervised study."

Mr. Serrano clearly is not happy that Ms. Deon is challenging him. He glares at her, barely concealing his contempt. "Student recommendations are an agreement outside of this matter and between the student and the teacher. It is clearly up to the individual teacher to accept or deny a request for a recommendation. I chose to recommend JT, but after his shameful treatment of one of our own staff members, I hardly think he merits my support. Whether I choose to stand by my recommendation or rescind it is entirely up to me."

I watch them stare each other down while Ms. McKay stares at her lap. Ms. Deon breaks the tension by saying, "We will continue this discussion at another time. If you'll excuse us, I have some items to go over with JT."

Mr. Serrano stands and nods to Ms. McKay who dutifully stands. She looks at me again and I say, "I really am sorry." She holds my gaze for a second then Mr. Serrano clears his throat and she looks away. They leave without saying goodbye, not that I was expecting a hug. Ms. Deon lets out a long slow breath, like my mom does after a particularly frustrating chat with me or Mamo. She's clearly rankled by Serrano and taking a moment to settle herself down.

Finally, she opens a folder in front of her and takes out a few pages. "JT, I made some screen captures of your Twitter account for my records and when I took some time to read through the messages something stood out." She slides the pages across the table to me. "Call it a hunch, but I don't think you were the person who wrote the tweets."

I glance at the top sheet and notice she's highlighted a couple of messages. One of them is about a super-cute graduation dress I saw online and the other is a comment about an ugly top some girl wore to school. I look up at her and shrug my shoulders. I can't even pretend to say I made the tweets. "Someone hacked my account. I've changed the password and deleted everything."

She raises her eyebrows. "That someone must be close to you, otherwise you wouldn't be covering for them." She takes the pages and puts them back in the folder. "Maybe you think it's a noble gesture to protect someone who would be expelled if they were caught bullying people on social media again. I happen to think that people never learn if they aren't held responsible for their actions."

I know she's giving me an opportunity to tell her the truth and get Serrano off my back, but I don't take it. I push my chair back. "I should probably get back to ISS."

Ms. Deon closes the folder and we both stand up. "I trust you can make it back without any side trips." I nod and she holds her hand up. "One more thing. If Mr. Serrano threatens you again, bring it to my attention immediately, do you understand?" I nod again and let myself out the door.

I pull out my phone and text Maddie on my way back to Room 114.

Meet me at lunch. We need to talk.

NINE
MONDAY BEFORE LUNCH

SERRANO IS NOT DONE with me. Not by a long shot.

He shows up right before lunch and straddles a chair in front of me again. His face does something that could be a smile, but I'm thinking it might be more of a grimace. One thing's for sure, he hasn't bought into the whole tooth-whitening trend. I don't know why I've never noticed before, but his teeth are coffee-stained and dingy. They remind me of the Indian corn you buy for Thanksgiving decorations, except the corn is more attractive.

This time he doesn't ask Jake to leave; he just pretends he doesn't exist.

"Unlike Ms. Deon, I wasn't impressed by your apology and I don't think your punishment is severe enough. If I ran this school, I would have doubled the suspension and put your behavior in your permanent record without a second thought." He tilts his head towards his shoulder and his neck makes a gross cracking noise. "If you ask me, this school needs to come down hard on *any* student insulting one of teachers and make an example of them."

I lean back in my chair, trying to get some distance from him. What happened to the guy that used to shake my hand and slap me on the shoulder when I aced a state exam? This side of Mr. Serrano is definitely a little unhinged.

He does that grimace/smile thing again and leans in closer. Jake clears his throat and the Wolverine looks up from his Manga reading and arches a fuzzy eyebrow at me. I'm so glad I'm not alone with this guy.

"You may be in luck, Mr. Monahan. I may have found a way for you to make up for your lack of good judgment." He leans back and studies me. "You seem to have a knack for tutoring and you clearly think your teaching skills are far superior to those of my staff, so I have a little proposition for you. We have a group of students that are, how shall we say it, underperforming in algebra. Perhaps you can use your *gifts* to help them master some of the concepts that they're struggling to comprehend."

I try to figure out where he's going with this. "Are you saying you'd like me to tutor some students?"

"That's precisely what I'm saying." He leans in even closer this time. "I'll make you a deal, Mr. Monahan. You work your magic with these students tomorrow and I'll reconsider my decision to write those letters."

At this point I'll pretty much agree to anything to get Mr. Corn Teeth out of my face. "I can do that. You know I'm a good tutor." Whatever it takes to keep him from sabotaging my acceptance to Stanford.

He leans back again. "Excellent." He shoots a look over to Wolverine and says, "Since one of the students is already here, I'll send the rest of the group down fifth period. I'll see to it that you have the whole afternoon to work with them. There will be ten students in all."

I notice his right eye is twitching a little. Mamo says that a sign for something, but I can't remember exactly what. I'm sure it's nothing good. He pulls a flash drive out of his shirt pocket and slides it across my desk.

"Use this to download the problem sets that you'll be using tomorrow. I'll send somebody down to pick it up in the morning and print out copies for you. Now write this down."

He gives me the username and password for a website and tells me to download five practice tests. I feel only slightly better when he leaves. Jake raises his eyebrows at me shakes his head as if to says he's sorry. Wolverine leans over and says, "That dude is seriously baked. What the hell did you do to get him on your shit?"

"Just some stupid Twitter thing. It wasn't even about him."

Wolverine smiles and nods. "Ms. McKay, huh? I saw that. You're right, she does suck. I got her for algebra. Worst teacher ever. I bet the rest of the kids he brings here are from her class because we aren't learning nothing." Jake tells us to stop talking and Wolverine goes back to reading comic books.

I pick up the flash drive and put that and the download instructions in my pocket. Wonderful, I get to tutor Ms. McKay's rejects. I'm not sure if this is a good thing or not. If I can help these kids understand a few concepts, then does that make me a good guy for helping Serrano keep his class averages up or a bad guy for making Ms. McKay look even more incompetent. Something tells me McKay isn't the one I have to worry about. Serrano is the one that's got me nervous and shaking.

TEN
NOT MUCH LATER ON MONDAY

I FLAG Miles down when I see him during our lunch run. He's chatting up Trish in the salad line, but he's not a salad guy, so I let him cut in front of me in the carnivore line. Trish watches him with a little dazed smile on her face. Looks like she's gotten herself smitten. He comes over and waggles his eyebrows at me. Looks like the smittening is mutual.

He looks back over his shoulder and makes puppy-dog eyes with Trish then turns back to me. "Trish says you got yourself grounded. Say it isn't so."

I roll my eyes, "My mother is being such a hard-ass. A month. Can you believe it. I'm going to miss the graduation fiestas. That is so cruel and unusual."

"Definitely harsh. Any chance she'll give you time off for good behavior? We ran into Allie at Pizza Hut on Saturday. Her graduation party is going to be massive. You have to be there."

"I'm working on it. I'll have to hire a lawyer to plead my case."

"What are you going to do about the concert next week? Trish has an extra ticket and she's asking me to go, but I'm not going to a Rockets concert without you. It's going to be X-chromosome central. I'll probably be the only guy there."

"Nah, there'll be plenty of guys hoping all their suffering will pay off in the back of their mom's minivan after the concert. Speaking of pay-off, how did your date go?"

He flutters his hand over his heart and pretends to swoon. "Rrrrowrrr, Trish is hot and she's a good kisser. Definitely a nine out of ten: soft, supple lips, minty fresh breath, and playful tongue action."

"Why only a nine?"

He gazes back at Trish and waves to her. "Slight nose whistle. I tried to block it out, but it was distracting." I try not to laugh. Miles is such a loser sometimes.

It's burger day, so I stack my tray with four of them, two milks and two chocolate puddings. I scan the lunchroom for Maddie, but don't see her anywhere. I'm surprised because she's usually with Trish who's waiting for Miles at our table. Jake has my phone locked up in a drawer, so I have no idea if she answered my text. She better not be dodging me or there'll hell to pay. I give up looking and walk back to Room 114 with Jake and Wolverine. I'll have to catch up with her after school.

I make a mad dash to Maddie's locker as soon as the last bell rings. There's no way I'm letting her go home before I talk to her. She's in a completely foul mood when she finally shows up five minutes later.

"Tell me you didn't blow me off at lunch time."

"No, JT, I was busy. For your information, I've had a horrible day."

"Well, it couldn't have been as horrible as having to apologize to McKay. You should have seen her; she was almost crying."

"Oh, for God's sake, tell her to put her big girl pants on and get over it already."

"Nice empathy, Maddie."

"Oh, please. She's a teacher, what does she expect? Kids are going to hate her. Time to grow a pair and man up."

"That's what you said about Jackie. Is that your answer for everybody you dump on?"

She looks at me like I'm speaking gibberish. "Of course. What's the big deal? It was just a stupid tweet. I didn't say it to her face."

"But it's the same thing whether you say it online or to her face."

"No, it's not. It's totally different. If I say it to her face, she has to listen. If I post it online, it not my fault if she reads it. Besides, it's a free country. I have my amendments."

"Are you even listening to yourself? What would happen if somebody posted some shit about you?"

"I'd kick their ass. Nobody's going to get away with that."

"OK, now remember that next time you want to post something nasty about somebody else."

"I don't get it. What's your point?"

I throw my hands up. "OH MY GOD, MADDIE. How can you not see your hypocrisy? Don't come to me when somebody wants to kick your ass. I just might help them."

"Some boyfriend you are. It's bad enough that you can't go to the concert on Saturday, now you're being so mean to me. Trish is going to give Darren's ticket to Miles and I'm going to be a third wheel, watching them molesting each other all night."

Way to change the subject, Maddie. "Hey, I told you I'm working on my mom. These things take time."

"Well, work harder. This is supposed to be my birthday present."

Now it's my turn to change the subject. "Speaking of Miles and Trish, I hear their big date went well."

"I suppose. Trish is such a slut."

"That's a little harsh. Miles said all they did was kiss."

She glares at me. "That's not what I heard, but whatever."

I give up; this stopped being a rational conversation ages ago. "You doing anything fun tonight?"

"No, just hanging out with my mom. Daddy has an open house."

I walk her to her car. "So, I never got to ask what you did on Saturday night? Hope it was more fun than watching *Lord of the Rings* with my grandmother."

She blushes a little and looks away, "Nothing much. Just went to the mall and got Chinese food."

"Anybody I know? Trish was obviously busy."

She starts to rummage in her purse for her keys. "Just Allie and some girls from the field hockey team. It was pretty boring."

She gives me a quick kiss and hops in her car. I step back so she doesn't run over my foot. My phone buzzes in my pocket. A text from Miles.

Coach says to see him before you run today.

My phone buzzes again.

Don't forget to ask your mom about grad parties. Need my wing man.

Wait a minute. Miles and Trish ran into Allie at Pizza Hut

not the Chinese restaurant. I look for Maddie's car, but she's already gone.

After dinner, I try calling Maddie, but she's not answering. I leave her a text message. Where the hell is she and why would she lie to me about being with Allie?

I try to download the problem sets that I'm supposed to do with the sophomores tomorrow. The first four take a couple of minutes each, but the fifth file keeps freezing my computer half-way through the download. I reboot my computer and try again, but get the same result. Damn cheap laptop. I'm so getting a new one with my scholarship money – that is, if I ever get any.

I try to think who could help me. Maddie could do it on her computer, but she would have to come over for the flash drive and there's the fact that she's not answering her phone. Miles could do it, but he lives two towns away and doesn't have a car. Most of the other kids I hang out with are useless when you really need something from them.

Maybe Helen. I can't ask her, but I'm totally screwed if I can't download the last file and Serrano is going to write that letter and I'll end up living at home the rest of my life because I can't go to college. I can't stay in Appleton; I'll die of boredom. I pick up my phone, but I don't have Helen's cell number because Maddie deleted it when she saw it in my contacts. Her parents got rid of their land line, so I'll have to go next door to talk to her. This is going to be painful.

ELEVEN
MONDAY NIGHT

I HAVEN'T WALKED the thirty yards from my front door to Helen's since our big blow-up last year. Going into her garage for a ladder is one thing, but knocking on the door and expecting to be invited in is a whole different situation. She hasn't forgiven me. Talking to me when she has to is one thing, but inviting me in to use her computer, in her bedroom, that's asking a lot, especially if you happen to date their worst enemy.

Crossing over into her yard is like that scene in the Wizard of Oz when Dorothy opens her door to her trashed house and the movie goes from black and white to color. Helen's yard is all sunshine and neat. Everything is pruned and green and flowers are already blooming. Not that my yard is black and white, but our house doesn't exactly look its best. Mamo used to be an awesome gardener, but along with the cooking, I've inherited the task of keeping our yard from looking like it's been abandoned.

I know how to prune and weed, but I just don't have the same touch she does when it comes to picking out flowers. My mother doesn't really notice the yard, so I use my own money to buy plants and try to make the place look nice. Last year I put the tall flowers in the front and the short ones in the back. This year I hope to do a better job. Maybe it would help if I read the little cards that come with the plants.

I climb up Helen's happy brick steps and take a deep breath and blow it out before I push the little button that ring the chimes. The door is red now instead of blue, but they still have the same lace curtains that Helen pulls aside to look out. She opens the door and looks me up and down, her eyes full of suspicion. I notice she's dressed in a skirt and a nice sweater and the silk scarf on her head matches everything. She even has nice make-up on, not the usual heavy eyeliner she wears to school.

"Well, look who it is. To what do I owe this honor?" Her voice drips sarcasm.

"Hey, um, I was wondering if I could ask you a favor."

"Maybe. Depends on what it is."

"I have to download this file and it keeps crashing my computer, so I was wondering if maybe you could help me."

She arches an eyebrow at me and says, "What is it? Porn? Sports Illustrated bikini photos? Something for Maddie's latest cyber-bully project?" Why does she always have to be such a wise-ass?

"Something for school. Math problems. Can you help me or not?"

She takes a deep breath and blows her grape bubble gum breath in my face. "I suppose. Come on in." I step inside the door, but can't help checking her out. She should dress like this all the time. She punches me on the shoulder. "Why are you staring at me like that?"

"I don't know. You look nice. What's the occasion?"

She rolls her eyes and says, "I'm sure there's a compliment buried in there somewhere. I just got back from dinner with my grandparents. My mom changed the menu at her restaurant, so we went to check it out."

I look around for a sign of her parents, but the house is quiet. "Are your mom and dad here?"

She turns to go up the stairs to her bedroom. "No, Mom's working and Dad's in North Carolina for some business thing, but don't get any ideas. You try anything and I'll send you home with your junk in a plastic bag."

Like I'm going to molest her bald self. "Don't worry, you're perfectly safe."

She stops half-way up the steps and glares down at me. "But you're not." She starts back up the stairs. "So, tell me again, what matter of smut are you trying to download?"

What does she mean, I'm not safe? I put a little more space between us. "Algebra problem sets." She looks over her shoulder and arches an eyebrow at me. She really is pretty when she wants to be. Scary and weird, but pretty. Too bad she's always so busy pissing the world off with her causes.

She takes a seat at her desk and points to a chair next to her. Her room is pretty much the way I remembered it. Amnesty International poster over her bed, old trophies and awards from her jock days, her half of our Spiderman walkie-talkie set still on her bookshelf. I wonder if her batteries are all corroded, too.

"I'm trying to keep Serrano from ruining my life." I don't know why I have to explain myself, maybe it's just to keep from having to deal with an awkward silence. "He's threatening to write to Stanford and the scholarship committees and tell them what a horrible person I am because of the stupid McKay tweet. If he does, I'm completely screwed."

She opens some program on her computer and says, "And

downloading math problems will somehow prevent him from ruining your life?"

"No, I had to beg and grovel for some way to make up for everything. He came up with this brilliant idea that if I tutor a bunch of sophomores tomorrow, he might cut me some slack."

She looks at me sideways. "You do know the state math exam is Wednesday, right?"

"Yeah, I guess that's the whole point. He wants me to do a help session before the test."

She spins her chair around. "Let me get this straight, somehow, in one day, you're going to miraculously make up for what his math department couldn't do in a year?"

"No, he just said they needed some extra help. He didn't say anything about them having to pass the test. That's ridiculous."

"I don't know. I'll bet you anything he's setting you up. These better be some magic math problems." She holds out her hand I give her the flash drive and the paper with the download instructions. Pink nail polish instead of her usual black. Who is this girl?

She plugs in the drive and types in the username and password and pulls up a folder with a bunch of files in it.

"I'm supposed to download five files. I got four, but the last one keeps crashing my computer."

"You still have that cheap-ass laptop from freshman year?"

"Yeah."

"No wonder. Time to upgrade, JT. Spend your money on technology instead of beer." She points to the screen and says, "This file is huge. What the heck's in it?"

We watch the little timer on the bottom of the screen slowly ticking away, predicting it will take twenty minutes to download the file. Even with her fast computer, the thing is a beast. Helen looks at me and says, "While we wait, do you mind if I ask you a few questions?"

I shrug my shoulders. It's not like she'll be quiet if I say *no*.

"First of all, are you a complete idiot?" OK, I was hoping for polite small talk, maybe about my grandmother or the weather. "Serrano is a bastard. He only cares about his precious math department and how good they look. Sure, you're super smart at math and aced the state math exams and all the other contests he made you enter, but you're graduating, so after next month you're useless to him. Second, why are you still taking the heat for Maddie?"

"What are you talking about?"

"Why don't you just rat her out? The girl's a menace to society. Why are you protecting her?"

"Because she's my girlfriend and if she gets busted for this she'll get expelled."

"When are you going to realize that Maddie and her goon squad are decidedly evil? How can you not see that?"

"She's not that bad."

"Well, sure, if you compare her to Ted Bundy or a serial child molester, but we're talking about the person who posted nude pictures of me online last year."

I look away, embarrassed that she might know that I looked. "They couldn't prove it was Maddie."

"That's because the local yokel police don't know squat about computers. I traced the files to her parents' IP address. I know it was her."

"How did *you* trace it to Maddie?"

She looks back at the screen to check the progress. "It's not that hard if you know what you're doing. I'm good with computers, you're good with math, Maddie's good at being horrible." She looks at her laptop and says, "Look, this is taking forever and I still have stuff to do tonight."

"OK, thanks for trying. Maybe I can use a computer at school." I hold my hand out for the flash drive, but she just laughs.

"Dude, I have to do laundry, but the file can download while I'm in the basement. Tell you what; I'll give them to you first thing tomorrow. Meet me in my driveway at 7:30 and I'll give you a ride."

"You don't have to give me a ride."

"Whatever, JT. You can ride with me or you can take the bus. I don't care either way." She stands up and smooths out her skirt. She even has nice, girl shoes on instead of beat-up boots or sneakers. I follow her downstairs and Helen stops and turns to me before she opens the front door.

She says, "Hey, you're going to Stanford, right?"

I shrug my shoulders. "Yeah, as long as Serrano doesn't screw everything up for me."

She says, "Cool. I'm going to Caltech. My aunt and I are taking two weeks and driving cross-country. We're going through San Francisco. You should come with us. Save yourself the airfare."

I stare at her, waiting for the punch line. Ten minutes ago, she was threatening to castrate me. "Why, so you can murder me and bury the body parts on some abandoned farm?"

She laughs and says, "I'm serious. You help pay for gas, share the driving, no harm will come to you. We're staying at campgrounds. You can bring a tent or use Gerhardt's pop-up bed."

"Wait, who's Gerhardt?"

She rolled her eyes at me. "My van. Gerhardt Wolfgang Von Vanagon, but I just call him Gerhardt."

"I thought cars were supposed to be named after girls."

"Gerhardt's a boy, why would I give him a girl's name? Anyway, the offer stands; you should come with us."

I don't look at her while I try to figure out a decent excuse. "I don't know. I probably should work right up to the last day of summer. I'll need the money." She's not surprised that I turn her down, but I feel bad anyway. "Which aunt are you going with?"

"Auntie Lin. The one you used to have a major crush on." She takes her scarf off and folds it neatly. I can't stop staring at her bald head. It's got stubble all over it, but it looks soft, not like scratchy beard stubble or Maddie's legs when it's time to shave them. I still can't believe she cut all her long, dark curls off. That was her best feature, except maybe for her brown-black eyes, which are watching me squirm.

"Is she going to be healthy enough to drive to California?"

"Yeah, she's totally kick-ass. Her doctors say she should be back to normal by the end of the summer." She's all bravado, but when she looks at me again, her eyes are tearing up.

"Tell her I said hello, if she even remembers me."

She swipes away a tear, smearing her make-up a little. "Tell her yourself next time you see her car in the driveway." She gives me a nudge with her elbow. "I'm serious. She always asks about you."

We say our goodbyes, but I stop before she closes the door behind me. "Hey."

"Hey what?"

"You should dress like that for school. You wouldn't get so much shit from people."

She laughs at me. "What you fail to realize is that I welcome the shit. Helps me separate the losers from the people worth dealing with." She pauses half a second. "In case you're wondering, I'm still holding out hope for you, John Taylor. Something tells me you haven't gone completely over to the dark side yet."

I wave my hand at her and jump down the steps. Fine. Don't take my advice.

TWELVE
EARLY TUESDAY

I WAIT for Helen by her ugly, brown VW camper van and shiver in the cold morning air. Typical Massachusetts spring. When is it going to warm up? The weather lady was all hyped up this morning about a Nor'easter coming on Thursday. I like watching her because she clearly loves her job. I've never seen anybody get so excited about rain. She's also into bicycle rights and knitting and all these crazy things that have nothing to do with the weather, but she's way better than the boring guy that did the morning forecast before her.

I look Gerhardt over while I wait. I don't feel any of my usual auto envy. I can't believe Helen drives this thing. Her parents have money, so they could probably buy her a decent car instead of this hand-me-down from her grandfather. We only have one car and my mother needs it for work. If she worked normal hours, I'd at least be able to borrow it to go hang out with friends, but I'm car-less and totally dependent on others for rides.

Helen comes out with no make-up, wearing a completely

hideous day-glo coral sweater with a sequined cat wearing a Santa hat and chasing a ball of yarn across the front. How can she look so pretty last night and go to school dressed like this?

I can't help myself. "Nice sweater. What'd you do, lose a bet?"

"No, I'm wearing it ironically to express my distaste for the typical high school girl's slavery to fashion." To tell the truth, I wish I had her cojones, but it's not like it doesn't come without a price. She holds up the flash drive and says, "That giant file that took so long to download is password-protected."

Helen tosses the flash drive to me and I stuff it in my pocket. Serrano didn't say anything about having to use a password on any of the files. I don't care. I downloaded everything in the folder like he told me to. If they're locked it's his problem.

I start to walk down the driveway. I have a few minutes before the school bus comes for my daily dose of humiliation. Helen yells at me, "JT, don't be such a loser. I'm driving to school. I promise not to murder you on the way." I turn and look at her. This is a tough decision. Helen with her heinous sweater and poop-brown camper van or a bus full of screaming underclassmen. I head back up the driveway. How bad can this possibly be?

I climb in the front seat and look around. I don't know what I expected, but it looks pretty much like a regular minivan, except it's got a little jump-seat behind the driver and a fold-down table. Helen rummages through a huge suitcase full of cassette tapes and pops one into the dash. She smiles at me and says, "Welcome to my mother's misspent youth. Poor Gerhardt is totally old-school, so you get to listen to her tapes from the olden days."

She hits play and blasts a band that I don't recognize. The

first song is angry and loud and I kind of like it. I wait until she's backed out of the driveway before I ask her who it is.

She stares at me like I'm brain-dead. "Really? You don't recognize the melodious voice of Joe Strummer?" I look at her blankly and she laughs out loud. "Joe Strummer, The Clash, only one of the best punk bands ever."

"You mean like 'Rock the Casbah,' that Clash?"

She lets out a little snort. "Well, yeah, if you want their later, more commercial stuff. This is their first album, the British import, not the American version that came out way later." She reaches over and pats me on the knee. "Poor JT, you've been listening to all that boy band crap with Maddie too long. Sit back and get yourself educated to some good music."

"I don't listen to boy bands." That's a lie because Maddie's been playing the Styrofoam Rockets' latest album non-stop.

We pull into the school parking lot a few songs later and I pick up the cassette case to check it out while Helen grabs her bag. She laughs at me again. "See, I knew there was hope for you."

I make a note to check out the rest of the album later and open up my door. "Thanks for the ride. Guess I'll see you around."

Helen shakes her head and laughs to herself. "Fine, I'll give you a thirty second head start. I wouldn't want you to catch shit from your friends for being seen with me."

I feel sort of bad, but it's true. Helen is an abuse magnet. I'd feel sorry for her if she didn't ask for it. Kids start with the wise cracks as soon as they see her sweater. I spot Maddie and Trish waiting in the courtyard by the front doors and pick up the pace to get further ahead of Helen.

Maddie finally responded to my texts last night, telling me

she was tired and going to bed. I swear she's avoiding me. Not cool, Maddie. I'll have to find a way to get her alone today.

I can tell from thirty yards away that Maddie has done something to her hair again. Her mom owns a salon and every few weeks Maddie tries something new: tints, feathers, extensions, whatever's supposed to be the latest hair trend. Her mom once offered to give me blonde tips, but I politely refused. This time Maddie got highlights, but something doesn't look right. They're way too light on her dark hair.

When I get close, she flashes me a big smile like everything is fine between us, but when she spots Helen walking behind me, her smile turns to a scowl. Maddie waits until Helen gets close and says, "Hey Helen, nice sweater. Did you mug some old lady at a bingo game to get it?"

Helen doesn't even miss a beat. "Nice highlights Maddie, but I think they looked better on the skunk that had them before you." Maddie's face clouds over and Trish has to stifle a laugh. Helen is gone before Maddie can come up with a response. She glowers at Helen's back then turns to us.

Trish says, "I told you they were too light."

Maddie ignores her and squints at me. "Tell me I didn't see you getting out of Helen's minivan. What were you thinking?"

"She's my neighbor. She gave me a ride to school. Maybe if my girlfriend got up earlier, she could pick me up in the morning."

Trish says she has to meet Miles before class and leaves me alone with Maddie. She steers me towards the hall with our lockers and says, "Did you have a chance to talk to your mom about the concert on Saturday?"

"No, she and Mamo were arguing all day and she was in a foul mood."

"Well, I was thinking, if you can't go, I'm going to invite somebody else, because Miles is definitely going with Trish."

I slip my arm out from Maddie's grip and stare at her. "Wait, I paid for the tickets. You just can't invite somebody else."

"They were my present. I should be able to use them any way I want, especially since you're totally bailing on me."

"I'm not bailing on you. I'm grounded because I covered for you for that stupid tweet."

"Jesus, keep your voice down. All I'm saying is I shouldn't have to sit by myself while Miles and Trish are all groping each other the whole night."

"Who are you thinking of asking? Whoever it is they should pay me back for the ticket."

"I don't know yet. I'm thinking about it."

"Well, stop thinking about it. Give me a couple more days to work on my mom, OK?"

"Fine. But you better talk to your mom soon. I'm not being some stupid third wheel."

The first bell rings and Maddie gives me a quick kiss on the cheek and runs off to homeroom. A kiss on the cheek? What am I, her aunt? I hurry down the hall to Room 114. Dammit, I forgot to ask Maddie about last Saturday night.

THIRTEEN
A LITTLE LATER ON TUESDAY

MR. SERRANO IS WAITING for me outside of Room 114. He holds his hand out for the flash drive and says, "I'll print out the problem sets and have them dropped off by the end of first period. The students you'll be tutoring will be here right after lunch. You'll have until the end of the day to prep them for tomorrow's test. Any questions?"

"Wait, I thought I was just helping them with some math problems. You didn't say anything about prepping them for the test."

"Maybe you weren't listening. These students need to pass the state exam that they'll be taking tomorrow and Thursday. I thought you wanted to make up for your bad behavior. If you've changed your mind, I can finish that letter I've been working on. I'm sure Stanford would appreciate being informed of how you show respect for your teachers."

Helen was right again. He's totally screwing me over. I remember what she said about one of the files. "Only four of the files opened. The fifth one is locked or something."

He gives me a funny look and says, "Nothing to worry about, Mr. Monahan, probably just a corrupt file. We'll have to make do with the other four. I'll see you after lunch."

Wonderful. Not only do I get to spend the afternoon tutoring struggling sophomores, now my life depends on them doing well. Maybe it won't be so bad. Not that I go around bragging about it at keg parties, but I've got a pretty good record as a tutor. Every kid I've worked with has improved by at least two grades. I don't count the soccer player that flunked geometry. She just didn't give a shit and never tried. Then again, I've never tutored ten kids at the same time.

Half an hour later, one of the student teachers shows up with eleven stacks of math problems. I start flipping through the first problem set and I notice a dark shape standing over me. Wolverine. He furrows his bushy eyebrows and says, "Are you really going to do this?"

"Yeah, I don't have much of a choice, do I?" He shrugs and I ask him, "What are the other kids like? Do you have any idea what they're having trouble with?"

"I don't know. It's probably the same kids she's always yelling at when we say we don't understand something. It's like she only has one way of explaining everything and if you don't get that, you're a total loser."

Jake clears his throat to get us to stop talking, but I say, "Give us minute, OK? I'm trying to help him with algebra."

Jake sits up and says, "Fine, but if I hear you talking about parties or girls, you're going to have to stop."

I turn back to Wolverine and tell him to sit in the desk next to me. "First of all, what's your name?"

"Alex, but everybody calls me Wolverine."

"Is that what you like to be called?"

He shrugs. "Sure, why not?"

"OK, what are you having the most trouble with?"

"It's the word problems. I can usually figure it out when it's just x and y, but if it's like cars and walruses I'm completely lost."

I spend half an hour working with Wolverine on word problems before he understands them enough to do them on his own. I give him the problem sets and have him do all the word problems he can find. I take the rest of the morning to go through the other exercises. Most of them are basic algebra and geometry. The state test isn't designed for geniuses. If you pay attention in class, you should get a passing grade. They do throw in some tricky questions once in a while to separate the better students from the average ones. I figure if I can teach these kids some basic problem-solving skills, they might have a chance at passing.

Jake escorts us to the cafeteria at lunchtime. He brought his own lunch, but my cellmate and I partake in the fine cuisine that the lunch ladies have slaved all morning to prepare for us. I get in the pizza line and five seconds later, I catch a flash of neon coral out of the corner of my eye. Helen. She gets in line behind me and pokes me in the back with a fork.

"So, what did Serrano say about that file?"

I give her an annoyed look and say, "Nothing much. He said it was probably corrupt or something."

She lets out a "Hmmmph," and says, "That's a load of

donkey turds. The file asked for a password. You think he's up to something?"

"Helen, not everybody is involved in a global conspiracy. Just forget about it, OK? I don't care what was in the file as long as Serrano gets off my back and drops his letter writing vendetta against me."

She leans over and looks in my tray. "Five slices of pizza? All that pepperoni is conspiring to clog your arteries with lard and cholesterol. Don't you know what's in that stuff? It's pretty scary."

I pick up the top slice and bite off half of it, chew a few times and swallow. "Mmmm, triglycerides. Lighten up Helen. I run over five miles a day. My cholesterol is fine. Now if you'll excuse me, I have to go educate some sophomores on the intricacies of basic algebra."

She starts to leave, but turns around and asks, "You want a ride home today? The rest of that Clash album is pretty awesome."

"Thanks, but I have to run after school. Coach is already pissed enough at me, so I can't blow it off."

She shrugs her shoulders. "Suit yourself. Good luck with the little ones. I'm sure they'll be eager to learn from you."

I watch her go sit by herself in the corner of the cafeteria. It's too bad she's usually such a pain in the butt because, when she's not on one of her soapboxes, I can remember why we used to be friends.

Mr. Serrano and nine sophomores are waiting for us when we get back from the cafeteria. So much for a relaxing meal. He introduces me and leaves the room. Wolverine gives me a thumbs up and Jake shoots me a sympathetic look. I'm sure he's run into these kids in gym class once or twice. Most of them seem fairly harmless except for a burly-looking girl with a ponytail, wearing a lacrosse sweatshirt with the sleeves cut off to show her well-muscled arms. She sits next to Wolverine and gives him a high five. I've seen them working out together in the weight room. She scares me more than he does.

I could have the kids introduce themselves, but I suck at remembering names, so I just start talking. "Mr. Serrano tells me you all need some help with algebra. Since I'm sure you're all in different places, I'm going to hand out a problem set and have you get started and I'll walk around and work with each of you individually." I pass out the first set of problems and get a chorus of groans. Lacrosse girl turns hers upside down and gets a few chuckles of approval. Wonderful. Bulging biceps and attitude.

"OK, here's the thing, as much as this sucks, it's only a few hours of your life. You're about to take a two-day math test. If you screw that up and fail, you get to keep taking it until you pass. So, you can let me help you figure this stuff out for three hours or spend the next two years taking the state test over and over again."

Lacrosse girl looks at me long and hard then flips her paper over and pulls a pencil out of her ponytail. I start with her first. She's actually got most of the basics down, but is having trouble with quadratic equations. I walk her through a few problems then move on to the kid behind her.

Three hours later, I collect the last of the problem sets and stack them on my desk. I look the kids over and say, "Any last questions?"

Lacrosse girl raises her hand and I nod my head at her. "What did you do to get stuck teaching us algebra?"

"I got in trouble for posting something online about a teacher."

She breaks into a smile full of braces. "You were the one that told Ms. McKay she sucked. Awesome. She totally does. You should be our teacher for the rest of the year. You're way better than her. I finally get some of this shit."

Jake says, "No swearing," but she knows she's not in trouble. The rest of the kids start laughing and talking.

The door clicks open and Mr. Serrano walks into the room. All the kids clam up and watch him walk up to me. "Well, Mr. Monahan; time's up. I trust these students will all be passing the state exam this week."

I hand him the stack of worksheets. "I did what I could."

"For your sake, I hope that's enough." The bell rings and he reminds the sophomores to get plenty of sleep and have a healthy breakfast tomorrow morning. Like that's going to make up for a year with McKay.

I grab my bag and head for the door. I've decided that I'll do my workout at home instead of here. I run into some kids from the track team who give me a hard time for skipping out on practice and end up missing Maddie at her locker. I run out to the parking lot just in time to see her Volvo pulling out onto the street. Crud. Now I have to run to catch the bus or I'll end up staying here until the late bus brings all the sports kids home after practices.

I'm sprinting across the lawn when I get a glimpse of neon and Helen yells at me. I remember the Clash album and skid to a halt. I cut across the lawn and meet her as she pulls her keys out of her messenger bag. She nods at me and unlocks my door then goes around to the driver's side. She starts up the car and pushes the tape back into the deck. Joe Strummer yells, "London's Burning," and Helen put the van in reverse. We don't even need to talk on the way home. Listening is good enough.

I lock my door and thank her for the ride. She just laughs and says, "Later, John Taylor." No sarcasm or guilt. I start to leave, but stop and turn around. "Any chance I could catch a ride tomorrow?"

"Sure. Don't be late or I'll leave without you." I run across the lawn. I'm either crazy or I've reached my school bus limit. Probably the first one.

FOURTEEN
TUESDAY NIGHT

MY MOM'S car isn't in the driveway when I get home. Hopefully she found the grocery list I left for her and is out picking up some food or we're eating cereal for dinner tonight. I open the door and the house is beastly hot. I check the living room for Mamo and she's in her usual spot on the couch, but she's only wearing her underwear.

"Jesus, Mamo, put some clothes on. Why is it so hot in here?"

"I was cold so I turned the heat up and now it's too hot."

I pick her pants and blouse up off the floor and hand them to her. The thermostat is set at 90, so I turn it down and open a window to let some of the heat out.

"Mamo, you had the heat way too high. Next time you're cold, put on a sweater."

She clucks her tongue. "You sound just like your mother."

"Speaking of mom, where is she?"

"I don't know. She was here a while ago." That could mean two minutes or ten hours in Mamo time.

I take a look in the kitchen and see partially unpacked groceries and a note from my mom. She got called in to work because somebody was sick. I guess we could always use the extra money, but I was hoping she could cook dinner tonight.

I put away the groceries and change for a run. The coach wants me doing sprints, so I jog down to the baseball field and do my workout to the sound of screaming Little League parents. When I get home, Mamo is asleep on the couch. I check my phone for messages. Nothing from Maddie, but I see three hang-ups from some number that looks familiar, but I'm not sure why.

That's the problem with programming people into my phone. I don't have to remember phone numbers anymore, just hit the name I typed in and it dials for me. Whoever it was didn't leave a message and since their number isn't saved on my phone, I doubt it's anyone important.

The house has cooled down, so I shut the window and wake Mamo up to ask her what she wants for dinner. I get her usual response: "Don't do anything special for me. Just give me whatever is about to spoil and I'll be happy."

"Fine, moldy yogurt and dry bread it is." I don't know why I bother to ask anymore. I check the refrigerator and decide to make stir-fry with chicken and broccoli. That way I can have leftovers for lunch tomorrow.

I'm in the middle of cutting up chicken when the doorbell rings. Mamo yells at me to answer it. She hates when anything interrupts her television viewing.

"I'm cooking. Can't you get it?"

"What's if it's the Jehovah's Witnesses?"

"Then tell them to go away." I hear her get up off the couch and go to the front door.

She yells, "It's a girl looking for you." Jesus, Mamo, give me something to work with, will you? I tell her to hold on and wash the chicken yuck off my hands and go to see who it is. The front door is wide open, but nobody is there, so I close it and look in the living room. Helen is sitting on the couch, watching the news with Mamo and going on about what a joke Congress is. What could she possibly want?

She doesn't say hello. "Don't you answer your phone? I called a million times." I notice she's wearing an ancient Luther Burbank Track sweatshirt instead of her hideous sweater. Helen is not a runner, so I'm guessing she stole the sweatshirt from her mom or her aunt. Both of them used to be big track stars back when they went to Burbank.

"That was you? I thought you were a wrong number. Next time leave a message or send a text."

"Well, save the number, so next time you'll know it's me. Anyway, I need to talk to you." She furrows her eyebrows and says, "In private. We've got problems."

Mamo picks up on this and says, "He didn't get you pregnant, did he? His mother got herself in trouble when she wasn't much older than you." Thanks for sharing, Mamo.

"No, Mamo, nobody's pregnant." I turn to Helen. "I'm in the middle of cooking dinner. Can this wait?"

"No, we have to talk." She follows me into the kitchen and pulls a chair up to the counter next to me. She looks around and says, "Since when can you cook? I thought boys only ate food out of boxes."

"I can do a lot of things you don't know about." I pick up my knife and go back to cutting up the chicken.

Helen leans on the counter and gets comfortable, like she's

not planning on leaving any time soon. "Word in the hallways is McKay kicked you out of AP Calc. You didn't tell me that. Kind of harsh if you ask me." I'm not sure I did ask.

"Yeah, Ms. Deon came to my rescue and wouldn't let her and Serrano flunk me. I have to finish the work on my own in study hall and Serrano will grade my tests."

"Speaking of tests, how did it go with the little ones? They all educated and ready to pass the state exam?"

I give her a hard look. "I did my best. I just hope Serrano keeps his end of the bargain."

"I don't know, JT, I hear he wants to make an example of you. You know, put your head on a pike outside the math office so no other kids think about insulting any of his staff members. You messed with a teacher. They have this mob mentality. Insult one of them and they all come after you."

I try to focus on cutting up broccoli and not my fingers. "Listen, Helen, no offense, but I got this under control. I made some pretty good progress with those kids today. I'm guessing they'll pass the test."

A little smile creeps onto her lips. "Interesting. He added that little stipulation to the deal, huh? I told you he would. You're totally screwed. Don't you get it? No matter how much butt you kiss, you're still going down. Ms. Deon can only help you out so much. Serrano is going to hang you out to dry."

I roll my eyes at her and stir the chicken in the wok. "Helen, please. Enough of your paranoid delusions."

"My delusions are not paranoid. I tell you something is rotten in the math department and it smells like Serrano. Did he say anything about that encrypted file?"

"I told you already. He said it was corrupt."

"He's lying. I tried to open it and it asked for a password. Corrupt files don't ask for passwords."

I put the knife down and stare at her. "If you don't mind, I need to finish cooking so I can feed Mamo and get her to bed at a decent hour."

As if on cue, Mamo comes tottering into the kitchen and says, "JT, is your girlfriend staying for dinner?"

"Mamo, this Helen from next door, not my girlfriend, and I'm sure she has dinner waiting for her at home."

Helen gives me a devious little smile and says, "Actually, I'm on my own tonight. I'd love to stay. Whatever JT is cooking smells absolutely delicious."

"Splendid. Now tell me, is JT behaving like a gentleman? Did he offer you a drink? Anybody want a little Jameson's?"

"Mamo, we're too young to drink." Helen snorts and raises her eyebrows. I raise my eyebrows back at her. I didn't say I *don't* drink.

Mamo says, "Nonsense, a little Irish whiskey is medicinal. Keeps you from going soft in the head." I take the bottle from her and pour her a couple of ounces over a lot of ice. Mamo isn't supposed to drink too much because of the meds she's on. The ice makes it seem like she's getting more whiskey than she is; a little bar tending trick I learned from my mom.

I hold the bottle up for Helen and she just laughs and shakes her head. Mamo tosses back her drink and holds her glass out for another. I give her another splash and put the bottle away on a high shelf.

Dinner conversation with Mamo and Helen is surprisingly normal. Helen catches us up on her sister and cousins and the latest news from her mom's restaurant. When the conversation comes around to colleges, Mamo catches me off guard. She's still picking up on more details than I give her credit for.

She looks me in the eye and says, "I know your mother wants you to go to school near here so you can live at home and take care of me, but I think a boy your age should have an adventure. You should go far away and do exciting things. Just don't get anybody pregnant and come back here to live with me. I'm too old to have any more babies running around the house." What's with the sudden obsession with pregnancy?

"Mamo, don't worry. I'm going to school in California and I'm not planning on getting anybody pregnant."

"You know, I wasn't a virgin when I married your grandfather. I had my share of lovers, but none of them made me feel like he did." She looks up at the ceiling, dreamy eyed. "He sure could melt my butter, but we always took precautions, no surprises for us. Now your mother; that's another situation altogether."

OH MY GOD, where is she going with this?

"Mamo, *way* too much information."

She plows ahead anyway, putting her hand on Helen's arm and leaning in close. "Do you know how JT got his name? His mom got herself drunk and did the mattress mambo in some guy's van after a Duran-Duran concert. Two months later I find her sitting on the toilet, staring at a pregnancy test. She didn't even know the fellow's last name so it wasn't like she could track him down. Anyway, when the time came, she named the baby after one of the musicians. Oh, she had herself a crush on that John Taylor. Posters all over her walls, writing his name on everything. She was obsessed."

Helen's eyes are wide with shock. Not even she knew this much detail about my sordid origin story.

"Mamo, enough! No more family secrets at the dinner table."

"Oh no, JT. Your girlfriend should know what she's getting herself into."

"Mamo, Helen is *not* my girlfriend."

Helen almost spits her food out from laughing. "Oh, Mrs. Monahan, JT and I wouldn't be a good match. He likes girls with big boobs and empty heads. You know, dumb, but fun."

"Well, you're certainly pretty enough. I can't say much for that haircut, but put a little make-up on and I bet you'll have my grandson breaking down your door."

Helen laughs out loud. "Thanks for the fashion advice. I'll keep it in mind if I ever need JT to break down any doors for me."

Helen stays to help me wash and dry the dishes. After we're done, I walk her to the front door, but she takes a detour to say goodbye to Mamo and thank her for dinner. When she finally makes it back to the door, I say, "You should be thanking me for dinner. I did all the cooking."

"Yeah, but your grandmother was the one that invited me." She grabs me by the shirt and pulls me out onto the front steps and closes the door most of the way behind me. "What are you doing for the next couple of hours?"

"Nothing, why?"

"Can you get out for a little while? Will Mamo be OK by herself?"

"No way, I'm grounded, remember?"

She lip farts and waves a hand at me. "Just tell your mom you had to come to my rescue. She'll totally buy it."

"I don't think so. I'm in enough trouble as it is. What do you need me for anyway?"

"It's a secret. The less you know the better, but I need a look-out."

"Then definitely not. I'm not getting roped into one of your crazy political stunts." I turn to go back inside, but she grabs my arm.

"Come on, JT, you owe me."

"How do you figure that? I just fed you. We're even."

She lets go of my arm and looks around. "Please, JT? Just for an hour. I promise you won't get in any trouble."

"No. Way."

"Fine, then I'll just have to write on my blog about a certain Duran-Duran concert, say around nineteen years ago."

I scowl at her. "That's blackmail and nobody reads your blog anyway."

She smiles at me. "All it takes is one person to spread a rumor, John Taylor."

Damn her. I don't need the world knowing I was named after some washed-up, frosted-haired, leather pants-wearing bass player from England. "Fine. When?"

"Give me thirty minutes, then meet me in your driveway." Jesus, I must be insane.

FIFTEEN
STILL TUESDAY NIGHT

HELEN IS WAITING at the end of the driveway when I open my front door. She watches me walk across the yard, revving Gerhardt's engine. Something's loose and rattles when she hits the gas.

I get in and she says, "Did you hear a noise when I was doing that?"

"Yeah, sounds like loose sheet metal. Is this thing going to blow up?"

"No, I think it's just a heat shield on the exhaust. I'll take care of it on Saturday." She puts the car in gear and pulls out onto the street. "You ready, JT?"

"Whatever. How long is this going to take?"

"Nice enthusiasm. Don't worry, I'll have you back in time to watch *Busty and Ignorant* or whatever reality show you're into these days."

I give her a withering stare and she just laughs at me, so I reach for the giant suitcase of tapes and unlatch the lid. She says, "How about some Replacements?"

"Who?"

"The Replacements. They're arranged alphabetically. Try *Pleased to Meet Me*. You should like that." I find the tape and pop it in and she's right; it's pretty good. Crunchy guitars, a raspy singer, and good lyrics.

We pull up in front of the little diner across from Luther Burbank and Helen backs into a space and shuts the van off. I look at her and say, "You hungry already? You just ate an hour ago."

"No, we're waiting and watching. If the local LEOs follow their usual routine, then we should see a patrol car in about five minutes."

"Local LEOs?"

"Law Enforcement Officers. Don't you ever watch NCIS?"

"Not unless I have to, but Mamo loves it. Do I want to know why we're waiting for the LEOs to show up?"

"No. Best if you don't. Your job is to call me if they come back while I'm doing what I'm doing. You got my phone number programmed yet?"

"No." She holds her hand out and I give her my phone. She pushes keys for a couple minutes and hands it back to me. She replaced Maddie as number one on speed dial with herself. I look for Maddie and she's number 666. Very funny.

I get a swat on the arm while I fix my phone. "Oooh, they're a couple of minutes early." I watch the cruiser turn into the school's driveway. "Now, once around the parking lots, get out and check the front doors, shine a light around the courtyard and then off to check the liquor store. These guys are so predictable."

We wait for the cruiser to finish its check then Helen grabs a dark canvas bag from behind my seat and says, "If they come back, call me. Got it?"

I shrug my shoulders and she takes off across the street, disappearing into the shadows of the pine trees along the student parking lot. I look around the van for something to do while she's gone and pick up the case full of tapes. There have to be around fifty cassettes inside. I turn on an overhead light and check out the band names. Most of them I've never heard of before: The Fleshtones, Hoodoo Gurus, Gang of Four, Human Sexual Response, The Del Fuegos, The The, New York Dolls, the list goes on. I recognize the Rolling Stones and Tom Petty and Elvis Costello – bands my mom listens to.

Mrs. Hernandez must have really been into music. Helen says she was a regular club rat, back when Kenmore Square was much scruffier and grimier. My mother says she didn't like going to clubs in the city. She went to concerts at Boston Garden or to the outdoor place in Mansfield (where Duran Duran played one fateful night).

A car pulls up next to me and I look up from the tapes. Crap. It's the police cruiser. The cop sits behind the wheel, fussing with something on the seat next to him and then looks up and directly at me. I have to will myself not to look away. I recognize him from security duty at football games and do a lame wave. He waves back and gets out of the cruiser.

Think. What if he asks why I'm sitting here? What do I tell him? I take a deep breath and look back, but he's gone into the diner. I look across the street for some sign of Helen, but seen nothing. She was wearing all black, so it's not like she would stand out anyway. I pick up my phone and look for Helen's number. Do I call her or just wait? What if the cop comes out when she's crossing the street? I decide to call.

She answers after a couple of rings.

"The cop's back, but he's in the diner. Where are you?"

"Just finishing up. Don't freak out on me JT."

"What if he asks why I'm sitting here all by myself?"

"Why would he care?"

"I don't know. Cops do that. They look for suspicious situations."

"Then don't look suspicious."

"I can't help it."

"Try not to wet yourself, will you? We didn't bring any spare pants. Go into the diner and order some coffee or something. Stop being such a putz."

"I'm not being a putz and I don't drink coffee."

"Then order a Fresca. I'll meet you inside. Take my keys, but leave the doors unlocked."

I hang up and take the keys out of the ignition then slip the tape case back under my seat. The cop is coming out of the diner with a cardboard tray full of coffees, so I hold the door for him then go inside. The diner is fairly quiet. Just a couple of old guys drinking coffee and eating pie. I grab a booth in the opposite corner and the waitress comes over with a menu. "We close in an hour, just so you know, hon."

She's not old enough to be calling me *hon*. Maybe it's mandatory waitress talk. She's got red streaks in her dark hair and a diamond chip in her nose and I can see tattoos peeking out from under her sleeves. I'm guessing she's in her late twenties and she probably went to Luther Burbank.

A couple of minutes later, Helen slides onto the bench across from me. The waitress smiles at Helen like she knows her and asks for her order.

"I'm just having coffee. Marissa, this is my neighbor, JT. JT, Marissa." Marissa arches her eyebrows at me, checking me out a little closer than before. She's pretty, but tired-looking. I'm guessing her life isn't very easy. Probably has a couple of kids at home and a husband that works long hours, too. Helen says, "What are you having? My treat."

"You got any iced tea?" Marissa nods and goes up to the counter. I look Helen over and notice her hands are dirty. She gets up and uses the bathroom, but when she gets back, she still has dirt under her nails. Now I'm curious. What was she burying or digging up at the school?

Marissa comes back with our drinks and leaves the check closer to Helen than to me. I watch Helen pour six containers of cream into her coffee. My mom and Mamo drink it black. I can't stand the stuff.

I mix some sugar into my tea and say, "So, will I be seeing you in Room 114 in the morning?"

She smiles at me. "Maybe on Wednesday. You should watch the baseball game tomorrow. You know they're in the play-offs, right. Should be a big crowd and Jimmy is pitching."

I take a sip of tea. She must have buried something in the baseball field. The bag she had was too small to be a nuclear warhead or a land mine. Besides, somebody would notice a freshly dug hole that big in middle of the field. It had to be something small and relatively harmless. Besides, Helen would never hurt anybody. She won't even kill spiders.

She takes a sip of her coffee, staring at me over the rim of her cup. She's got ridiculously long eyelashes and her brown eyes are looking almost black tonight. "So, JT, tell me why you picked Stanford. I heard you got into Harvard and Dartmouth. Don't you want to stay near your beloved Maddie?"

"It's a good school. Why'd you pick Caltech?" She doesn't need to know I'm going to break things off with Maddie before we go to college. Long distance relationships never work. Besides, I could use a little less drama in my life next year.

"Because they have an awesome computer department and it's as far away from small-town Massachusetts as I could get and still have decent weather."

I try not to laugh because I picked Stanford for pretty much the same reason.

"My aunt Clare went to Stanford. She loved it there. She gets all misty-eyed when she talks about it. It's not a party school, but you should have fun. There's lots of stuff do around Palo Alto."

We sit there for a couple of minutes drinking and watching the old guys argue about the Red Sox. I ask her, "Are you coming back to Appleton after college?"

She shrugs her shoulders. "I don't know. Maybe. Depends on if I go to grad school or where I get a job. I could end up in northern California or Seattle or maybe get a job in Washington, DC. You never know. What about you? You coming back?"

"No."

"No, as in never?"

"No, as in I'm not coming back to live here. I might visit once in a while."

She arches her eyebrows at me. "What about Mamo? I thought you guys were pretty close."

"We are. It's just that things are changing. She won't really be herself much longer. I mean not the real her. The Alzheimer's is progressing pretty quickly. She'll probably be in a home before I'm done with school. She already forgets who I am some days. I don't think I can deal with her not knowing me at all." I look at Helen again. Why is she so easy to talk to? I never talk about serious things with Maddie.

"I'm sorry. I love Mamo. She's a pisser, as my Auntie Lin

would say." She's quiet for a moment. "Remember that time she caught us scarfing down her bag of chocolate? She was furious."

I laugh out loud. We ate a whole bag of her chocolates while we were watching a Star Wars marathon a couple of years ago; didn't leave her one little square. Unfortunately for everyone, it was her last bag. Mamo does not do chocolate withdrawal pretty. She had to go cold turkey all afternoon and night because my mom had the car.

"Oh my God, I swear she was beating down the doors of the grocery store the next morning, waiting for them to open. Do *not* mess with Mamo's stash, *ever*."

I catch her staring at me. "What?"

"Nothing."

"No, why were you staring at me like that?"

She shakes her head. "I was just remembering something, but it doesn't matter. We should get going. Don't want you turning into a pumpkin."

Helen finishes her coffee and I leave the last of my iced tea. I'm not really thirsty anyway. I slide her keys across the table and fish a couple of dollars out of my pocket. Helen shakes her head at me. "My treat." She leaves a big tip for Marissa and we drive home, listening to The Replacements and not saying anything. When she pulls up in front of my house she says, "Remember, stop by the game tomorrow. I figure between the sixth and seventh innings would be a good time."

"I'll do that. If the cops ask me any questions, I'll plead the fifth."

She cracks up. "Always good advice. Have a lovely night, JT. Sweet dreams."

"You, too. Hope your delusions don't keep you up." She gives me a punch on the arm as I get out. I watch her park and make sure she gets into her house without being carried off by wolves or angry villagers.

When I get in, I check the caller ID on the land line. No calls from my mother. Mamo is zonked out on the couch, drooling on a throw pillow. All is well in Appleton. At least for the moment.

SIXTEEN
EARLY WEDNESDAY

THE WEATHER LADY is completely off the dial this morning. She's got tracking maps, three different weather models and the latest 3-D graphics going non-stop for the Nor'easter that's supposed to arrive tomorrow night. She's predicting it will hit central Massachusetts with heavy rain and high winds sometime after dinner and last through the night. I'm not worried. I plan to be safe and dry at home watching crappy TV shows with Mamo.

    Helen is idling Gerhardt in front of my house when I open the front door. She rolls the window down and yells, "Hurry up. I have stuff to do before homeroom." I climb in and some crazy-sounding guy is talk-singing and telling me not to eat stuff off the sidewalk. I catch her eye and say, "What. Are. You. Listening. To?"

    She smiles at me and says, "The Cramps," then crosses herself. I stare at her until she explains. "Just a little prayer for Lux Interior, the lead singer. May he rest in peace."

    I raise my eyebrows at her. "Let me guess, he ate something

off the sidewalk." She laughs and calls me a blasphemer. She tells me all about the band for the rest of the trip to school. The next few songs are equally weird, but cool at the same time. Helen calls it psycho-billy. If you ask me, it defies description, but I still like it.

When we get out of the car, Helen says, "I'll pretend to tie my laces while you get a head start. Just be forewarned, keep your skunk on a leash or I won't be responsible for any verbal abuse I lay down on her." I take in her outfit and shake my head. Black jeans, a really ugly rainbow shirt from the 70's or 80's, a scuffed-up pair of Doc Martens and a vintage ski vest in brown and rust stripes. Instead of a scarf, she's got a red and white polka-dot bandanna on her head. Where does she find these things?

I wave and head for the school, glad to get some distance between myself and her fashion nightmare. Maddie and Trish are in their usual spot and I herd them to the front door to avoid any scenes. Maddie just looks at me and says, "You got a ride from her again? What are you some kind of sadist?"

"You must mean masochist."

"No, sadist, you know, a person that tortures himself all the time. Why are you driving to school with her? Have you lost your mind?"

I don't bother to correct or answer her. "Hey, I've been meaning to ask you something. Who did you hang out with on Saturday? I'm just curious because…"

She interrupts me. "Did you talk to your mom last night?"

"No, she had to work." I try to continue my interrogation. "You said you had dinner with Allie, but Miles said she was at McDonald's."

"But you promised you'd ask your mom about the concert."

"And you said you'd give me a couple of days. I'll call her

tonight at work. So how could Allie be at the Chinese place and McDonald's at the same time?"

"I didn't say I was with Allie."

"Yes, you did. You said you went to the mall with her and went out for Chinese."

"Well, you must have heard me wrong."

The bell first rings and she rubs my arm and backs away. "I have to go. Make sure you talk to your mom. I need to know, OK?" Before I can say anything, she turns and runs down the hall, skunk stripes flying in the wind. An arm rub? What the hell was that and why is she changing her story about Saturday? I know I heard her say Allie.

Wolverine is taking the math test, so it's just me and Jake in ISS today. I spend the morning catching up on the work I couldn't do yesterday. How can I have so much homework when I'm not even in class? When lunchtime rolls around, I have to make the trip down to the cafeteria because Helen ate my leftovers-to-be last night and I have to buy lunch again.

Turkey, mashed potatoes and cranberry sauce are on the menu. Definitely a three-lunch day. Miles and Trish are in line, so I cut off a couple of freshman girls with a smile and an apology. They blush and don't complain; works every time.

Miles fist-bumps me. "Dude. Turkey day. Hope you're hungry."

"Is a frog's butt watertight?"

Trish furrows her eyebrows. "What kind of answer is that?"

Miles says, "Allow me to explain. A frog spends most of its life in a pond, so in order to survive it needs to regulate how much water enters its body. With that information, you can hypothesize that its butt must be watertight, therefore JT is hungry."

"Why can't you just say yes?"

I poke her on the forehead and she swats my arm away. "Because I love to mess with your brain. So, Miles, what's the update on graduation parties?"

Miles shakes his head. "Man, you better make peace with your mom or you're going to miss out. I count at least five epic events so far, including Allie's, and two of them are pool parties and you know what that means: babes in bikinis."

Trish gives Miles a smack on the arm. "Hey, both of you will be keeping your eyes to yourselves. No leering at other girls allowed." I've seen Trish in a bikini. I don't think she'll have any trouble keeping all of Miles' attention. He rubs her shoulder and they start doing cute talk. I have to turn away to keep my gag response in check. I scan the lunch room, but don't see any sign of Maddie. Where the hell is she? I swear she's avoiding me.

I make my way through the crowd balancing my lunch on a tray and Helen pulls up beside me. She peers at my food and says, "Jesus, JT. How can you eat so much and still be so scrawny?"

"I'm a growing boy."

She rolls her eyes and peels off to her lonely corner, but not before she reminds me to watch the end of the baseball game. I almost forgot about that. I'll definitely work it into my schedule.

SEVENTEEN
WEDNESDAY, AFTER SCHOOL

SINCE I STILL CAN'T PRACTICE WITH the team, Coach tells me to do a distance workout. Run the three-mile cross-country trail twice, alternating 100-yard sprints with a fast jog for half a mile. Sounds like fun.

I don't mind running by myself. It helps me think about things and I have plenty to think about. Why is Maddie avoiding me? How did the kids I tutored yesterday do on the test today and what about tomorrow? I need them to do well. I think I got through to most of them. If lacrosse girl was getting it, then I must have been doing something right.

I come out of the woods along the athletic fields and hear a cheer come up from the baseball game. Somebody got a hit. I see the center fielder from the visiting team running towards me, chasing a ball. By the time he gets it back to the infield, the Luther Burbank player is standing on third base. Kids and parents are hooting and clapping and carrying on. Helen was right. There is a big crowd today.

I check the scoreboard when I come out of the woods the

second time: top of the fourth, tie game. I have time for a quick shower before the end of the sixth inning, when whatever Helen buried last night will reveal itself. The track team comes in from practice while I'm dressing and I get tons of abuse about being a slacker. Yeah, right. I saw most of them lounging around the high jump pit while I was doing my work-out. Coach never works them too hard the day before a big meet. A meet I'll be missing because of Maddie.

The bleachers are packed with parents and students, so I look for a place to sit on the slope overlooking the right side of field. There are a few students there, but nobody I know, so I sit by myself. I scan the bleachers for Helen, but don't see her bandanna or bald head anywhere, so I get comfortable and watch the game.

The score is still tied going into the bottom of the sixth. Burbank gets a leadoff double and an error allows the second batter to get onto first, but the other team's pitcher strikes out the next three, leaving runners on first and third. Bummer.

Jimmy Driscoll gets back on the mound for the final inning. Rumor has it he's already being courted by a school in one of the Carolinas. He's doing his warm-up pitches and the infield is tossing the ball around, when I hear shouts from the crowd. It doesn't take long to spot what the commotion is all about.

Directly behind second base, a giant neon-pink balloon is inflating itself. The players stop tossing balls and both the benches and the people in the bleachers stand up to get a better look. The balloon is huge, maybe five or six feet in diameter with something written on it in big black letters. I get up and move closer so I can read it. I *cannot* believe that girl.

DON'T LET
BREAST CANCER STEAL

SECOND BASE.

The balloon deflates after about thirty seconds and the umpires rush over to take it away. From where I'm standing, I can see a small divot in the ground and a flap of grass to the side of it. The second baseman flips the grass clump back with his toe and stamps it down and shrugs his shoulders. One of the umpires takes a quick look and tells the coaches to settle their teams down. I see Ms. Deon standing up and scanning the crowd. She's got to be looking for Helen, but she's nowhere to be found.

My phone buzzes and I pull it out of my pocket. Guess who.

"Who's winning?"

"The score's tied. Where are you?"

"Home. Making brownies."

"Ms. Deon is here. I think she was looking for you. Want me to tell her you say hello?"

"No, but thanks anyway. Did it work? What did the crowd do?"

"Yeah, it worked and you got a pretty good response. People are still laughing."

"Cool." She starts talking about how brownies from scratch are so much better than the stuff from a box, but I cut her off.

"Wait, how did you know when to set it off if you're home in your kitchen?"

She laughs and says, "Sorry, but that's top secret. If I told you, I'd have to kill you." She hangs up and I spend the rest of the game trying to figure out how she pulled off her prank. It had to be someone sitting in the bleachers, but who? Helen doesn't have any real friends except maybe Jimmy and he was on the mound, warming up. How the hell did she do it?

Jimmy shuts the other team down with fourteen pitches and then he hits a sacrifice fly to score a runner from third base, winning the game. He gets soaked in Gatorade for his efforts and is carried off the field by his teammates. I hang back and listen to the parents as they walk towards the parking lot. Most of the conversation is about Jimmy Driscoll, but the rest of it is about the giant pink balloon. I guess Helen got their attention.

I spot Ms. Deon with the balloon folded up and tucked under her arm. She sees me and waves me over. Her face is a mix of school pride and curiosity. I say, "Good game, huh?"

She smiles at me and says, "Yes indeed, they made it to the semifinals."

We walk a few steps together and Ms. Deon says, "You didn't happen to see Helen at the game, did you? I know you two are friends, so I thought I'd ask."

I shake my head. "I know she went home after school. She's probably there now, picking out something ridiculous to wear for tomorrow." That gets a laugh from Ms. Deon. I point to the balloon and say, "You think that she had something to do with that?"

She smiles at me. "Let's just say I might have a few questions for her."

"Want me to tell her you were looking for her?"

She smiles and says, "No, I'm sure I'll see her in the morning. You have a good night, JT. One more day and you're free." She says goodbye and heads back into the building.

I scan the crowd for Jimmy's parents to see if they'll take pity and save me from a long bus-ride home. I don't see them, but a woman about their age is waving at me. She steps closer and says, "JT! It's been forever. Look how tall you are." She takes her sunglasses off and then I recognize her: Helen's Auntie Lin. She's got a Patriot's cap on, but I can see shiny scalp underneath. She gives me a hug and puts her sunglasses back on. "It's good to see you. You should come over and say hello next time I'm visiting."

I promise I will and stop her before she leaves. "If I were to check your phone, would I happen to see a call to a certain niece about twenty minutes ago?"

She laughs and touches the brim of her cap in a salute. "I plead the fifth. See you around, JT."

The late bus is full of rowdy baseball players. I sit in front and pull out my phone to text Maddie.

We still need to talk.

Ten minutes later:

Can't tonight shopping with my mom tomorrow I promise

I've barely talked to Maddie this week. Between her "busy schedule" and me being grounded and in ISS, I haven't seen her for more than twenty minutes total. It's Wednesday night; we've usually sent a million text messages by now and had at least one make-out session. Is she mad at me? Is she truly that busy? Who the hell knows?

EIGHTEEN
EARLY THURSDAY

I'M sure that if they filmed the weather lady below the waist this morning, she'd be wearing waders. She's predicting near apocalyptic rain tonight. She's got all the weather graphics going overtime like there isn't any other news to tell. When I walk down to the end of my driveway, there are hardly any clouds in the sky and other than still being too cold for my taste; it looks like it's going to be a nice day.

Without thinking, I turn up Helen's driveway and stand near Gerhardt. Helen comes out a couple of minutes later, wearing a fluorescent pink, page-boy cut wig. She's got heavy eye make-up on with the liner sweeping out to the sides. When she sees me, she acts like it's perfectly normal to look like Cleopatra with fake pink hair.

"Where the hell did you get that?"

"Little shop I know in Cambridge. Cool, huh?"

"No, not really. Looks like something you need to keep away from open flames."

"I'll try to remember that if I come across any raging

infernos." She smiles at me. "How's it hanging? Life treating you well today?" Not really, but I'm not telling her that. She unlocks the door and I climb into the seat and immediately reach for the tapes. I would have spent the night stressing over how weird things are getting between me and Maddie if Mamo hadn't created a distraction.

Helen plucks a tape out of the box and pops it in the dash. "Two Tone ska mix tape, rude boy. I think you'll like it." She back the car out of the drive and slaps me on the arm. "What's bumming you out, JT? You look like someone peed in your Cocoa Puffs."

I'm not sharing my Maddie woes, but I *can* talk about my grandmother. "Mamo had a bad night."

"I'm sorry. Is she OK?"

"She's fine. She's oblivious, but fine." I think about how much I should share. Maddie never wants to hear bad news, but I think Helen is honestly concerned. I take a deep breath and let it out slowly. "Sometimes Mamo falls asleep on the couch; well actually she's always falling asleep on the couch. Anyway, when she gets into a really deep sleep, she doesn't notice things like maybe that she has to go to the bathroom."

Helen grimaces. "She didn't. Not on the couch?"

"No, at the last minute she got up and ran to the bathroom, only, as you know, Mamo doesn't exactly move fast. She shuffles off and a few minutes later, she comes out with nothing on below her waist."

Helen bursts out laughing. "No way, you mean totally bare-assed?"

"YES! Except she's coming at me, not walking away. I didn't look away fast enough, so it's burned into my memory. I can't un-see it."

Helen's jaw drops. "Hokey smokes, Bullwinkle. You mean grandma half-frontal nudity. Yikes."

"Yeah! So, I ask her where her pants are she says, 'They got wet, so I left them on the floor.' Then she starts heading back to sit on the couch!"

Helen cringes. "What does 'they got wet' mean?"

"It means there was a huge puddle on the bathroom floor with a soaking wet pair of pants, granny underwear and slippers and socks in the middle of it. I had to turn her around and make sure she cleaned herself up and put dry clothes on and then I had to clean the bathroom and wash her clothes. Oh, and then I took a shower. A long one."

She shakes her head, pink Barbie hair flopping back and forth. "God, JT, you're a verifiable saint."

"Yeah, and the road to heaven is paved with granny pee." I look her in the eye for along second. "You do what you have to do. If it was your grandmother or your Auntie Lin, you'd do the same thing."

She shrugs her shoulders. "I suppose I would, but I hope I never have to."

"Speaking of Lin, I saw her at the game last night. I know she and Jimmy's mom are best buds, but I'm wondering if she was there for another reason, maybe something to do with a giant pink balloon?"

Helen gives me some side-eye and laughs, "Sometimes you're too smart for your own good, JT."

We listen to the tape the rest of the way to school. It's sort of like the Mighty Mighty Bosstones that my mom plays sometimes, but the accents are British and Jamaican, not Boston. It definitely sucks you in. I pick up the tape cover and scan the band names written in her mom's tiny block letters:

The Specials, The Beat, Selecter, Madness. Never heard of any of them, but that doesn't mean I'm not liking it.

When we get to the parking lot, I wait for Helen instead of running ahead of her. I have questions about the ska stuff and she's more than happy to answer them. Maddie and Trish are nowhere to be seen, so we walk into the school without incident. Helen gets a crack about her wig from some punk junior in the hallway, but I tell him to shut his yap. I leave Helen at her locker and cruise by Maddie's, but see no sign of her so I head for ISS. Maddie's disappearing act is getting annoying.

Wolverine is still taking his math test, so I nod to Jake and pull out my world history book and notes. I haven't touched them since last week, so I need to do some major cramming today if I want to ace the test tomorrow. I'm just settling in when my phone buzzes in my pocket. Jake has his nose buried in another magazine, so I check my messages. Helen.

    Shit is hitting the fan big time. We need to talk at lunch.

Jake is still reading so I write back.

    ????

    - I'll ask the questions. Just meet me at lunch.

Wonderful. God knows what she wants now. Maybe I'll skip lunch today.

I don't skip lunch. I'd be dead of starvation by two o'clock. Cleopatra Barbie is waiting for me by the entrance to the cafeteria and follows me to the sandwich line.

"I can't stay and talk, you know. I have to get back as soon as I buy my lunch."

"Ask me how my morning went, JT."

"How did your morning go, Helen?"

"It sucked big time. Ask me why, JT."

"Why did your morning suck big time, Helen?"

"Because Ms. Deon and the head of the state testing board wanted to know why I downloaded files from that website. *Apparently*, the locked file contained answers to the state math exam and *apparently*, somebody at the testing facility was selling the answers to teachers and *apparently*, the state was monitoring the site to catch whoever downloaded the files, but since I downloaded them onto a flash drive that you gave to Serrano, I have no way to prove that he made you download the files for him."

"They can just ask him for the flash drive and if he has it, then he's busted."

"Yeah, like he'll admit to having stolen answers. Do you have any witnesses that saw you give him the flash drive?"

I think about it. Jake and Wolverine weren't at Room 114 when I gave it to Serrano. It's my word against his. "Um, that would be a no."

"So, right now, for all the state knows, I downloaded the file and sold it to the highest bidder and I'm guilty and I'm going to cheating jail."

"There's no such thing as cheating jail."

"How do you know? It could be some secret FBI facility that nobody knows about. One morning I'll drive off to school and a black van full of jack-booted test police thugs runs me off the road and POOF, I'm gone. Nobody ever hears from me again. My mom and dad will have to put lost daughter posters up all over town and cry themselves to sleep at night." She's talking so fast that she's not breathing and droplets of her saliva are spraying from her mouth and landing on my shirt. Vile.

"Helen. Take a deep breath. You're hyperventilating and you're spitting and it's kind of gross."

"I'm going away to cheater prison for the rest of my life because of you and you're worried about a little spit?"

"How is this all my fault?"

"Let me illuminate you." She starts counting off on her fingers. "A- You didn't have the balls to rat out your evil girlfriend; and B- You didn't have the sand to stand up to that ass-wipe Serrano; and C- You're too cheap to buy a decent computer, so I got stuck doing the download for you."

"Fine, I'm a horrible person. I'll make a note to hang myself tonight."

"If only it were that easy."

"Listen, I have to go back to ISS. I'll try to figure something out and get back to you, OK?"

"No, it's not OK. You need to figure out what Serrano wanted those files for. If he's cheating or he sold them, you need proof. Got it? I will not allow you to screw up my life, Monahan. You are not off the hook until I am free and clear of this stinking mess." She pokes me hard in the chest and spins on her heels, stomping her way to the salad line.

Shit. Maybe she's just being paranoid or maybe not, but the whole thing is pretty freaky. How did they know she downloaded the files? What if her website tracking story is real? I downloaded files. Are they after me, too? Are the test police really watching us? I look around the cafeteria. Everything looks normal, but maybe *too* normal. Now I'm getting paranoid.

Suddenly, I'm not very hungry. I only buy three sandwiches.

NINETEEN
THURSDAY AFTERNOON

I SPEND the first part of my afternoon studying for my world history test and trying to come up with some sort of a plan to prove Serrano is cheating. If he *is* cheating, I have no idea how or where he would do it. How do I prove a teacher is cheating when I'm stuck in a room all day with no contact from the outside world? The more I think about it, the less I think I can do anything. Helen's whacked. There are no cheating police. She's innocent until proven guilty. They have no proof that she sold any files or even that she gave them away. The whole thing is a figment of her paranoid imagination.

I watch the clock slowly tick its way through fifth period, but I still jump when the bell rings. Two minutes later, Helen walks into Room 114.

She turns Jake and says, "Ms. Deon asked me to drop off some of JT's assignments. They're kind of complicated, so I'll have to explain them to him."

Jake looks her over and figures she's legit. As legit as a bald girl wearing a pink wig can be. He says, "You got five minutes while I hit the head. No shenanigans, OK?"

As soon as Jake closes the door, Helen pulls up a chair and sits across from me. I slide my chair back a little. I need some room to maneuver if she goes for my jugular. "Here's the deal. You have until eight o'clock tonight to figure out your plan."

"What happens at eight o'clock?"

"That's when Serrano leaves the building. The tests end at two-thirty, Ms. Deon has a staff meeting from three o'clock until five and then parents' night starts at five-thirty. If Serrano is going to do anything, he has to do it after the conferences. My guess is he'll go off-site because it will be too obvious to stay here. The tests get picked up first thing in the morning, so if he's going to do anything it has to be tonight."

"What am I supposed to do? I can't follow him. I don't have a car."

"You have a girlfriend, don't you? She has a car. Get her to help you. Reach down way deep inside yourself and grab a fistful of cojones and stand up to her. Jesus, Serrano could be screwing up your life forever and I'm getting dragged in along with you all because of her stupid tweet."

Jake comes back from the bathroom and tells Helen she should get back to class. She dumps a stack of papers on my desk and says, "I have to meet with Ms. Deon, the head of the state testing board and the superintendent of schools tomorrow morning. Don't let me down, JT. I know where you hide your spare key. You are not safe."

She leaves and I look down at papers she left for me. They're handouts from the nurse's office about head lice, teen pregnancy and sexually transmitted diseases. If Jake had looked and any of this stuff she would have been screwed. Where does she get the nerve to do what she does?

Serrano stops by to terrorize me twenty minutes before the last bell. This time, he doesn't ask Jake to leave and he doesn't sit backwards in a chair, he stands over me and glares at the pile of handouts on my desk. Normally, I'd try to explain them, but I'm beyond caring what he thinks.

He says, "Just a quick update for you, Mr. Monahan. Based on their reactions at the end of the day, it looks like the students you tutored fared well on yesterday's portion of the state exam. However, today's test was much harder. I sincerely hope for the sake of your college career that they do equally well today."

I'm really beginning to not like this guy. He thinks he holds all the cards and can ruin my life at will. The problem is, he does, so I have to play nice or I'm screwed. Serrano gives me a superior smirk and leaves the room and Jake says, "You want me to tell Ms. Deon that he's been harassing you?"

I shake my head. "No, I'll be fine," but I probably won't be.

I stare at the books in my locker and try to comprehend how miserable my life has become all because Maddie can't keep her comments to herself. Five days of ISS is punishment enough, but Serrano comes along with his personal vendetta, now Helen is sucked into the mess and threatening to do physical harm to me. With my luck, the whole thing is going to blow up and leave no survivors, except of course for Maddie and Serrano. This is so unfair.

My phone buzzes in my pocket. It's a text from Maddie.

Did u talk to ur mom last nite

I don't even bother to answer her question.

You have pick me up at seven and help me do something tonight.

- Why its supposed 2 rain

I need a ride to a couple of places.

- Sounds boring why don't u ask ur new girlfriend

Would you rather I had a chat with Ms. Deon?

- U don't need 2 be like that

Bring your camera and fill your gas tank.

- Why do you need my camera

Because the one on my phone has a cracked lens. Don't be late. Gotta go.

- Love U 2

Sorry, Maddie, time to pay back some of your debt.

TWENTY
THURSDAY EVENING

I TELL Maddie to pick me up at seven o'clock because I need her to actually be at my house by seven-thirty. With Maddie, I always build in extra time. I feed Mamo, make sure she's had her meds and is settled on the couch with something she likes on TV. I have homework I could be doing, but I'm too jumpy to sit still.

Maddie picks shows up at 7:35 and glares at me when I climb into the SUV. "JT, I still have homework. This better not take long."

"Did you bring your camera?"

"Yes."

"Did you charge the battery?"

"I'm not stupid. You're lucky I could even find the charger. I haven't used this thing since I got my new phone." She pulls her pink digital camera out of her purse and hands it to me. "You still haven't told me what we're doing."

"We're going to spy on Mr. Serrano."

"Why on earth would you want to do that?"

"Because I think he's going to cheat on the state exams and I need to get proof."

"I can't believe you dragged me out on a school night to spy on a teacher. You know I can't get in trouble. It's bad enough that Serrano is all over your case, I don't need him on mine."

"Since when do you care about being out on a school night? Last week you and Trish stayed at the mall until it closed."

"We were shopping for graduation dresses. That was totally essential."

"Well, this is totally essential to me. If I don't get proof that Serrano's cheating, then I won't be able to go to Stanford."

"Fine, but this better not take long."

We drive over to the school and wait in the teachers' parking lot. One thing about driving a Volvo is you blend in with the teachers' cars pretty well. We scrunch down in the front seats and I watch Serrano's car while Maddie spends her time texting and talking on the phone. Parents' night ends at 8:00, so we shouldn't have to wait that long.

I pull out the camera and figure out how to turn it on. The little battery icon is half full, so I should be OK. I make Maddie take a break from her gossip-fest to show me how to use it.

"Honestly, JT, you need to get up to speed with the rest of the world. Digital cameras have been around forever." She gives me a quick run-down and I test it out on her. She sticks her tongue out and gives me the finger. What a sweet girl.

"Is the memory card full? How many pictures can I take?"

She rolls her eyes at me. "I don't know, enough. I haven't used that thing since last year."

I shut the camera off and go back to watching the parking lot.

Maddie says, "I'm not waiting any longer, by the way. I'm going to find somebody else to go the concert with me."

"Why can't you just wait?"

"Because I know you. You're never going to talk to your mom and you're going to call me at like five o'clock on Saturday and tell me you can't go."

"What's so bad about going with Miles and Trish?"

"I'm not being some stupid third wheel."

"Fine, then who are you going with? The same friends you were with last Saturday? I know you told me you were with Allie, but she was at McDonald's with Miles and Trish."

She squints at me. "I told you. I wasn't with Allie. You were mistaken."

"Yeah, whatever, then who are you taking to the concert?"

"I don't know. Somebody."

"Well, you must have somebody in mind. Tell me who it is? One of your field hockey buddies? Hannah? Rachel? That one with the bad dye job, what's her name, Sophie?"

She turns and glares at me. "Sophie gets her hair done at my mom's salon. It's not bad."

It is. It's a strange pale yellow, with blotches of darker yellow that remind me of a urine sample. I'm beginning to wonder if someone at her mom's salon needs a refresher course at beauty school.

"Whatever. Whoever it is, she better pay me back. The ticket isn't free."

"Um, news flash, JT, they're my birthday present. I can do what I want with them. Just because you got yourself grounded doesn't mean I have to suffer."

I turn and glare at her. "News flash for you, Maddie. You got me grounded with your stupid tweet."

"I told you it was an accident. I can't believe you won't forgive me already. That is so unfair, JT."

I want to scream or punch something. Why is she being so dense? I tell myself to count to ten and pay attention to the parking lot.

A couple of minutes later, Serrano and McKay walk out of the building together and head for their cars. Maddie's inability to grasp the obvious is suddenly not important anymore. Serrano pulls up next to McKay's car and says something through his open window. Hmmm, maybe his little sidekick is coming along to help out. I give Maddie and elbow and tell her to start up the Volvo.

"Who am I following?"

"Serrano, I guess. His bag looked like it was pretty heavy. They're probably going somewhere now to do their dirty work."

Maddie makes a face and says, "If they go to some motel and have sex, I am so not staying." She does a little shudder. "Teacher sex should totally be outlawed."

They don't go to a motel. Serrano goes to McDonald's drive-thru and heads towards his house. I know where he lives because one of our long-distance training runs goes down his road. It's an ugly, flat-roofed modern architecture job in the middle of the woods. Kind of like the one Ferris Bueller's buddy Cameron lived in, except I doubt there's a vintage Ferrari in the garage.

We drive past Serrano's house and I spot McKay's car in the driveway next to his. Serrano is in the middle of a messy divorce, so I don't expect his wife to be around. The word in the hallways is that he got caught bisecting the acute angles of a student teacher at a math conference last year. Maybe Maddie is right and he and McKay are hooking up. I am so *not* getting pictures of that.

I tell Maddie to drive about fifty yards down the road and pull over in between houses. I check the camera and open the door. Crap. As the weather lady so passionately predicted this morning, it's starting to rain. A lot. I pull my hood over my head and tell Maddie to wait for me.

"How long is this going to take? I still have homework to do."

"I don't know. Stay off your phone. I may need to call you for back-up."

"No way. I flat-ironed my hair today. I'm not going to go running around in the pouring rain."

I glare at her and say, "Stay off the phone," then shut the door and run down the road towards Serrano's house. I should have worn boots instead of my old Vans because they're soaked as soon as I cut across the lawn. The driveway is lit by floodlights, so I stick to the overgrown bushes near the house. I creep around, peeking in windows.

I don't see anything from the front of the house, so I go along the side, getting soaked by wet bushes and rain dripping off the roof. The rain gets heavier and the wind starts picking up. I imagine the weather lady getting all giddy with climatological nirvana right about now.

The ground slopes downhill towards the back of the house so the windows are above my head. I grab the ledge of a likely candidate and pull myself up high enough to peek in. I can see Serrano and McKay sitting at a table with piles of answer books in front of them and a couple of McDonald's bags. It must be his dining room. There's a big sliding glass door behind him that looks like it opens onto a deck.

He pulls out a folder full of acetate overlays and hands half of them to McKay. Helen was right; they are going to change the answers. My fingers start slipping, so I look around for another way to catch them in action. Maybe if I climb one of the trees or better yet, maybe I can sneak up onto the deck and get a good shot.

I creep towards the back of the house, and trip on a garden hose and land on my butt. Crap. My ass is soaked. I'm brushing leaves and mud off my jeans when I hear a door slide open and Serrano says, "I don't know. Maybe it's a raccoon. Something's out there and he's going to keep bugging us until I let him out." I freeze. Toenails and paws thud on the deck overhead. I look up and a huge dog is looking through the deck rails at me. He lets out a loud woof and takes off for the stairs.

Holy crap. I didn't even think about a dog. I run for the nearest tree and jump for a low branch. I grab on and pull myself up just as the beast comes tearing around the side of the house. I've never climbed anything so fast in my life. The problem is, my old beat-up Vans are slippery on the wet bark.

The dog looks up at me growling and drooling. Jesus, he's huge. He looks like some kind of mastiff or maybe Serrano is secretly breeding dogs with hippos in his spare time. I climb up higher and find place that I can sit and think. I still need some kind of proof. I look through the branches and get a glimpse of part of the dining room table. All I can see is man hands and answer books.

Serrano opens a page and lays one of the acetate sheets over it then lifts it up and starts erasing wrong answers and filling in correct ones. I try to take a picture, but I can't balance, hold the camera and move branches out of the way with only two hands. The hound from hell is sitting in the mud staring up at me and doing a low growl. This isn't going to work. I need a distraction.

I pull my phone out and call Maddie. She answers after it rings a million times.

"You done yet?"

"No. I told you to stay off the phone. I'm stuck in a tree and there's a huge dog and I need you to help me."

"Oh no. I'm not going anywhere near huge dogs. JT, this is stupid. Just come back and let me go home. I'm tired and I have to pee."

"Are you not listening? I'm up in the tree and there's a dog waiting at the bottom of it. This thing is massive. I need you to make some sort of distraction."

"JT, it's pouring out there. I don't have an umbrella. My hair is going to frizz."

"Maddie, rain is soaking through all my clothes, I've got a major tree branch wedgie and there's a giant dog waiting to maul me as soon as I try to get down. I don't give a shit if your hair frizzes. Do something to help me."

"Someone's on the other line. Hold on." I wait for an eternal minute then Maddie gets back on. "That was my dad. He wants me to be home in five minutes or I'm grounded."

"He's bluffing. Your parents have never grounded you."

"He's really mad this time. And I have to pee. JT, I have to go. I'll call Trish. Maybe she can come pick you up." Maddie hangs up. SHE HUNG UP. I can't believe she hung up. I hear her car start and then see the lights come on. I watch her drive by and disappear in the gloom. SHE LEFT ME. She left me in a tree, soaking wet with a giant dog waiting to eat me. And now I have to pee. Damn you, power of suggestion.

TWENTY-ONE
LATER, ON THURSDAY

I LEAN against the tree and blink the rain from my eyes and try to think of what to do. I look down and Cerberus is standing with his paws on the lowest branch. He hooks his front legs over it and starts to climb. Dogs aren't supposed to climb trees, but after a lot of grunting and huffing, he's standing on the branch looking for a way to reach the next one. Wonderful, it figures Serrano's mutt would be half dog and half orangutan.

I hiss at him to go way and he looks up at me and lets out a long, low, rumbling growl. Nice doggie. He gets his balance and puts his front paws up on the tree trunk. This is crazy. He might actually be able to reach me. I look around for something to throw at him, but all I have is my phone and the camera and I need both of those. Then I get a brilliant idea and take off one of my shoes and throw it at him.

It bounces off his skull with a *thunk*, but he keeps growling at me and looking for a way to climb up onto the next branch. I need to do something soon or I'll either die of exposure and bladder failure or get eaten by a mutant tree-climbing dog. Or both. Stupid Maddie. If she hadn't mentioned pee, I probably wouldn't have to go. Now I'm about to burst. I look around but it's not like I can go behind a bush to relieve myself. I'm stuck. I look down at Brutus and an evil idea creeps into my brain. Wretched dog. I'll teach you to climb trees.

I unzip my jeans and lean a little to the left and relax my cramped bladder muscles. The stream of pee lands a few inches away from Cujo's head and I adjust my aim and hit him between the eyes. You wouldn't think something that big could move so fast. He starts barking like crazy and hurls himself against the tree trunk. The only problem is that he forgets he's in a tree and lands on the ground with a thud. I adjust my trajectory and hit him in the face a couple of more times before I run out of ammunition and he goes completely insane.

It takes him a couple of minutes to wear himself out. His bark is all hoarse and he's panting and coughing. I glare down at him through the branches and loud-whisper, "That's what you get, Marmaduke." He settles himself in the mud and starts eating my shoe. Damn, I was hoping maybe Serrano would call him in because all that barking would annoy neighbors off, but they're probably too far away to hear anything.

I close my eyes and shiver as cold water runs down my back. How can this possibly get any worse? Ten seconds later I get my answer. Lightning. I see a flash and a loud boom follows a few seconds later. Wonderful. That was less than a mile away. More flashes light up the sky and this time they're closer. I'm high up in a tree in the middle of a thunderstorm. I think the weather lady would agree that this is not a good idea.

I hear the door slide open between thunderclaps and Serrano starts yelling for the dog. "Skipper. SKIPPER. COME BOY. SKIPPER COME. NOW."

Skipper? Who names their dog after a character from *Gilligan's Island*? Serrano grumbles and comes out onto the deck. I can barely see him through the leaves and torrential rain, so I'm hoping he can't see me. "Skipper. Leave the damned raccoon alone and come now before you get hit by lightning." The dog lets out a couple of more barks then scrambles up from the mud and heads back to the house. Luckily, Serrano trained the beast.

I hear the dog on the deck and then listen for the door to slide shut. I climb back to where I can see in the window and check on their progress. I see Serrano dry his hands off with a napkin and pick up another test booklet. He's only got a couple left in the pile. I have to get the hell out of here, but not without proof.

I take a tentative step out on the branch, holding onto a clump of leaves and twigs. My shoeless foot has good traction, but my sneaker is slipping and sliding. I lean out as far as I can and hold the camera out. I can see Serrano clearly, test books, acetates, erasers and everything. I push the button, taking two pictures with the flash going off. He looks up for a second, but lightning flashes, lighting up the whole sky and he goes back to fixing the tests.

I turn sideways and edge myself closer to the tree trunk and check the results. I'm not going to win a Pulitzer any time soon, but the pictures aren't half bad. I turn the camera off and shove it in my pocket, then pull out my cell phone.

I call Maddie and she picks up on the first ring. "The dog finally went inside. Come pick me up."

"I can't. My mom and dad won't let me go back out in the storm. It's really raining hard and there's thunder and lightning, you know."

"Really? I hadn't noticed."

"You don't have to be so sarcastic. I have to finish my homework. I'll see you at school tomorrow."

"Maddie! I'm in stuck in a tree at Serrano's house. You have to sneak out and pick me up. It's like five miles from my house and I only have one shoe."

"This was your stupid idea. Why do I have to save you? Can't you call Miles?"

"No, I'm not calling anybody else. I wouldn't be here if you hadn't gotten me in trouble in the first place. You owe me, big time."

"I can't believe you're going to hold one teeny little mistake over me for the rest of my life. That's so unfair." I hear her cover the phone with her hand and muffled shouting in the background. "My mom is yelling at me. I have to go." She hangs up on me again. I call her back and she says, "What now?"

"Maddie! I. Need. A. Ride. You can't just leave me out here."

"JT, I told you, I. Can't. Leave. My. House. Call your girlfriend, Helen. She's always giving you a ride. Maybe she'll come pick you up in her Turd-mobile"

"Maddie. You owe me. Come get me now!"

"Now my dad is yelling at me. I have to go. Bye." She hangs up and I stare at my phone. You suck Maddie. You really, truly suck. I send her a text message.

> You completely suck. I never should have covered for you.
> - If u bring that up 1 more time I'm breaking up with u.
> I want a divorce.
> - Fine by me have a nice life loser
> Have fun getting expelled.

I stuff my phone in my pocket and it buzzes at least three more times in the next minute. Get bent, Maddie. You only give a shit when you stand to lose something. You can sweat it out tonight wondering if I'm going to rat you out or not.

I start to make my way down when a flash lights up the whole sky and an ear-splitting boom follows it almost immediately. I drop the rest of the way to the ground and start running. I'm halfway up the driveway when I remember my shoe. I run back, stubbing my toes on bare roots and squishing through mud and who knows what else. My shoe should be at the base of the tree, but I don't see it anywhere. Damn you, dog from hell.

The front door opens, so I dive into some bushes for cover. I slither around in the muck and listen to Serrano and McKay prattle on about how bad the storm is and how she should get going before it gets any worse.

This is a Nor'easter. It doesn't get a whole lot worse than this, people.

McKay makes a dash for her car and I wait in the mud until she backs out of the driveway. I roll over onto my back and pull my phone out of my pocket and notice the battery icon is blinking. Enough power for one more call. I punch in Helen's number and she answers on the second ring.

"Hey, I was wondering if I could ask you for a favor."

"I don't think so. The last time I did a favor for you, I got interrogated by state officials."

"Helen, please, I need a ride. I don't know who else to ask."

"Where's Maddie? Why can't she pick you up?"

Another bolt of lightning lights up the sky followed immediately by a deafening crash of thunder. My phone starts beeping or maybe it's my ears ringing. Helen says, "Where are you?"

Before I can answer, my phone dies. Maybe I'll just lie here and let myself drown.

TWENTY-TWO
STILL THURSDAY

I START WALKING. With one shoe. With a dead phone. With a very strong suspicion that Maddie may not have been the best choice I could have made for a girlfriend. I'm about a mile down the road when I see headlights through the rain. I don't want anybody to recognize me, so I pull my hood down over my face and step off the road into a ditch full of rushing water. Rocks and cans and God knows what else bang past my ankles as I wait for the car to pass me. Instead, it slows down and a familiar voice yells out, "Get out of the ditch and into the car, you moron." Helen.

I open the side door and slide it closed behind me then lie down on the floor in the back of the van. She turns on an overhead light and looks me over. "On a crap scale of one-to-ten, you look like a solid eleven. I was going to tell you to sit up front, but maybe not."

"Thanks, but I think I'll just lie here and die."

"Try not to get too much filth on my rug, OK? I just vacuumed this car."

I notice the song booming over the speakers near my head. "What are you listening to?"

"*Rain* by The Cult. I thought it was a good choice for tonight."

I tilt my head and listen to the lyrics. "Did he just say, *hot sticky sins?*"

"No, I looked it up. The lyrics sites say it's *scenes*, but *sins* would be way cooler. OK, just two questions. You better have the right answers or I'm tossing you back in that ditch. Did he cheat and did you get any proof?"

"Yes and yes." I curl up into a shivering ball and ask her to turn the heat up. Helen turns off the light and twists some knobs on the dash, then puts the car in gear. We're in my driveway ten minutes later. I sit up and look over at Helen. To her credit she doesn't laugh at me.

"Can I see the pictures?"

"Sure, why not?"

I hand her the camera and she curls her lip at the pinkness of it. "Nice camera. Very manly. All you're missing is a *Hello Kitty* sticker on the back."

"It's Maddie's."

"I have the same model, only in black. Do you have the cable or the software to download the photos?"

"No."

"That's a problem." She hands it back to me after taking a quick look at my handiwork. "Come over around seven tomorrow morning. We can download the photos to my computer and print them out. We're going to need to show these to Ms. Deon and the testing guy."

I get out of the van and wait on my front steps until Helen is safely inside her house before I open my front door. I take one look and almost turn around and run back out into the storm. The living room is a disaster area and Mamo is huddled on the couch like a scared kid, my Little League bat clutched in her hands.

When she sees me she starts sobbing. "Close the door, JT. You'll let them in."

"Let who in?"

"The killers. They're out there."

"What are you talking about? There's nobody outside." I approach her slowly, looking around the room, taking in the destruction. The front door is dented and one of the lamps is broken.

"What happened to the door?"

"They were trying to get in, so I beat on it. I think I scared them away, but they said they were coming back."

"Who, Mamo? Did you see them? What did they look like?"

"No, but I heard them. They were talking to me. They told me to hide because they were coming to kill me, but I scared them off." She's had paranoid episodes before, but never like this. My mom says bladder infections can make old people act crazy. I'll have to remind her to get Mamo to her doctor for a test ASAP.

I talk to Mamo in a calm voice while I take the bat from her iron grip. I notice she's shaking, so I take the afghan off the back of the couch and put it around her shoulders. Her hands are bruised, but when I look them over, I don't see any serious cuts. "Mamo, listen, I need to take a shower and get some dry clothes on. Are you going to be OK for ten minutes?"

"What if they come back?"

"I'm here. I'll take care of them." She reaches for the bat, but I tell her I'll protect her.

I take a quick shower and throw some sweats on then go

back to check on Mamo. She's zonked out on the couch, so I wake her up. "Time for bed." I make sure she cleans up and gets into bed then I do what I can with the living room. I can't do much about the dents in the door. It's metal, so she must have been wailing on it like a mad woman. I guess I should be glad we don't have glass in the door like Helen and Maddie do.

The phone rings, so I pick it up.

"Where have you been? I've been calling all night." Crap. Busted.

"Ma, it was an emergency. I had to go out."

"I don't want to hear it, JT. They're closing the bar early because of the storm, so I'm heading home. Don't even think about going to bed." She hangs up and I flop down on the couch. Something soaks into my sweats, so I jump up and check out the couch cushion. It smells like pee. This was the spot Mamo was sitting on when I came home. Double crap. Now I need to take another shower.

To say my mom is furious is a major understatement. I'd rather be back up in that tree with the rain and lightning and a mad dog waiting to munch on me than face Hurricane Ma. When she sees the damage Mamo did to the living room and front door, she gets apoplectic, blaming me for not being there to stop her. Why is it my fault that my grandmother had a psychotic episode?

"You should have been home, JT, not out farting around with your friends. What if she had hurt herself?"

"Ma, I wasn't out farting around. I had to do something."

"What was so important that made you go out in the middle of a storm when you're supposed to be grounded?"

"It's complicated."

She looks at her watch and stares me down. "I've got all night, JT."

I tell her everything, the download, the tutoring, Serrano's threats, the state testing guy grilling Helen, how Serrano and McKay were changing answers, Skipper, the tree-climbing dog from hell, Maddie abandoning me. I don't leave anything out.

When I'm done, she says, "Why didn't you tell me earlier?"

"Because you always tell me I'm supposed to take care of my own problems, not come running to you."

"JT, that's for the little stuff, not state testing boards and psychotic teachers. What if you had fallen out of that tree and broken your neck? What if that dog had bitten you? I'm going down to that school first thing tomorrow and having a word with that Serrano character. Nobody threatens my boy and gets away with it."

"Ma, I got it covered, OK? I got Helen for back-up and she's like a computer genius. She's going to figure out a way to prove everything." Actually, I'm just making that up, but the last thing I want is my mom showing up at school and ripping Serrano a new one. I wouldn't put it past her to kick him in the crotch if he gave her any grief.

"Well, I can't just sit here and do nothing." She puts her hand down on Mamo's wet spot and pulls it away immediately. She sniffs her palm and looks at me. "Tell that's not what I think it is."

"It is. We have to talk. Mamo is getting worse. I don't think she can stay by herself anymore."

"Why do you have to go to school so far away? If you went to a local school, you could live at home and help me with your grandmother while I'm at work."

"You need to get a babysitter. I showed you that ad I found.

You should call that lady and check her out. She sounds really nice."

"Nice and expensive. What about that college in town?"

"You mean the religious college that closed down two years ago?"

"Oh yeah, well, there's Fitchburg State and the community college in Worcester. What about those?"

"No. Absolutely not. Besides, I didn't apply to those schools. The whole point of college is to get away from home."

"I thought the point was to get an education."

"Yeah, well that, too, but mostly to do it far away." She scrunches her brows at me. "Ma, I am going away, no matter what. I'm not staying here. Mamo needs help. I don't think we can leave her alone anymore, not even for a little while."

She gets up to wash her hands then comes back and sits in the armchair across from me. She looks defeated and tired. "It's not supposed to be this way, JT. Your grandmother is too young for this. Alzheimer's is for people in their eighties, not sixty-eight. It's not supposed to progress this quickly, either. Nothing is the way it's supposed to be."

"Ma, it is what it is. We can't control everything. You weren't supposed to get pregnant and drop out of college. Helen's aunt wasn't supposed to get breast cancer. I'm not supposed to be in trouble for Maddie's stupid tweet."

She rolls her eyes at me. "You could have controlled your mess. You should have turned that girl in the minute you knew it was her."

"Yeah, but I couldn't because I care about her."

"Do you still care about her after tonight? After the way she left you stranded?"

I shake my head. "I don't know, Ma. I don't know."

"Well, I want you to think about that. I don't think she

really cares about you. At least not the way she should. You deserve a lot better than her and that's not just your mother talking. You ask your friends. Ask Helen. You'll see." I already know what Helen thinks.

My mom gets up and stands over me, arms folded. "Go to bed, JT. It's late."

"What about Mamo?"

"I'll take her to the clinic in the morning and have her checked for a bladder infection and I'll make some phone calls. I might have to get that woman in to watch her a couple of hours a day until we figure things out."

"We have to have it figured out by the fall, before I go away."

"I know, JT. I promise I'll take care of it." She runs her hands through her hair and lets out a sigh. "I know I shouldn't do this, but I'm going to let you off for Saturday night. You can go to your concert, but you're still grounded for another three weeks after that."

I stand and straighten up to my full height and force her to look up at me. She hates that I'm eight inches taller than her puny five-foot-four. "Do me a favor, just let me off so I can go to the graduation parties."

"What about your concert?"

"I don't think I want to go anymore and Maddie already has plans to go with somebody else. The band kind of sucks, anyway. Kind of like a modern-day Duran-Duran."

She spins me around and gives me a hard shove towards my bedroom. She may be a runt, but she's a strong runt.

TWENTY-THREE
EARLY FRIDAY

THE WEATHER LADY says the storm is over Nova Scotia and heading into the North Atlantic. I walk outside and it's sunny and warm for a change. We have branches and pine needles all over our lawn, but the only thing that leaked in the house last night was Mamo. I'll be spending the weekend cleaning up the yard, but I don't care. I'm free. No more Room 114. No Styrofoam Rockets concert. But, I still have to deal with Maddie and Mr. Serrano. Maybe I'm not so free after all.

I ring Helen's doorbell and her mom lets me in. She and Helen's dad are eating breakfast and I can hear Helen upstairs. If her parents are surprised to see me, they don't show it. I make small talk with her mom about her restaurant and try to picture her as a little club rat, punking out in Boston back when she was in college. I can't see it. I've always known her as a mom.

Helen yells at me to come upstairs and shows me how to download the pictures from the camera while she finishes getting ready. The software lets you scroll through thumbnails of everything on the memory card, so I check them out while the pictures print.

Most of them are of Trish and Maddie and their friends. They're all from last year. I keep looking to see if there are any good shots of me. Not really. I take horrible photos. My eyes are closed or I'm not smiling or I'm looking in the wrong direction. I'm about to give up and shut the camera off when I see a photo that makes me sit up straight. It's from just after we first started dating. I scroll and find two more just like it. I cannot believe this. I shut the camera off and take a deep breath. Maddie lied to me. The whole time she lied to me. I can't believe it. I can't believe I trusted her.

Helen comes back into the room and sits on her bed while she pulls on a pair of scuffed black Blundstone boots and rolls her jeans just enough to show the tops of them when she's standing. She's got a black bandana with skulls on her head and a vintage t-shirt from another band I haven't heard of: Scruffy the Cat. I arch an eyebrow at her and she smiles and says, "I stole this from my uncle. They played around Boston back in the 80's. Kind of a roots rock, country sound. I have a tape in the car."

She squints at me and says, "You OK? You look a little pale. You're not worried about today, are you?"

"No, I'm just tired. I was up late last night."

"Everything OK with your grandmother?" I lie and say she's fine.

She looks me over like she doesn't believe me, but she gets up and takes the photos out of the printer. "They're kind of blurry, but you can tell it's him."

"So how is this going to work? Do we just go see Ms. Deon when we get to school?"

She shakes her head. "I'm supposed to meet with her before lunch. Why don't you meet me in the cafeteria after?"

"You don't need me to be there?"

"No, we better keep it simple. You're in enough trouble as it is."

"But what about you?"

She smiles and picks her up messenger bag and slips the photos into a pocket. "Piece of cake, JT. Ms. Deon and I go way back."

"That reminds me. What ever happened with that big pink balloon. Did you get busted for that?"

She smiles at me. "I'm not at liberty to discuss the case while it's still being investigated. Come on, we better get going. Don't want to be late for your first day of freedom."

When we step out of Helen's house, I spot Maddie's car idling in my driveway. It's nice to see that she can get herself out of bed early if her life depends on it, but I'm not ready to deal with her yet.

Helen looks at me and says, "Your girlfriend is here and something tells me that's not her happy face." Helen waves hello and Maddie gives her the finger. Nice manners.

I don't bother to wave. "Yeah, and it looks like she's got her panties in a major twist, too. Do me a favor, if I don't show up for physics, call the state police and have them drag the river."

Helen says, "My advice is to stay out of kicking and spitting range. If you have to, go Jerry Springer on her ass and hit her with a folding chair. That usually takes the fight right out of them."

"Thanks, I'll keep that in mind."

I pat my pocket to make sure I have the camera and walk across my lawn. Maddie is clearly battling to keep Good Maddie from being taken over by Evil Maddie. Her knuckles are white on the steering wheel, but she gives me a scary, tight-lipped smile that reminds me of Jack Nicholson as the Joker.

I open the passenger door and lean in. "Hello dearest, to what do I owe this pleasure?"

"Just get in, JT. I'm not in the mood for your humor."

I climb in and close the door. "Good to see you, too, Maddie. Now really, why are you here?"

"Because I don't want to break up with you." She puts the car in gear and backs onto the street. "Can we just forget about the fight last night and go back to normal?"

There is no normal after what I found on her camera, but I'm not ready to deal with that yet. "I don't know. I'm kind of pissed that you left me stranded."

"Fine. I'm sorry. I'll make it up to you." The sincerity scale barely registers a three, but I'm curious to see where she's going with this.

"How?"

She turns and glares at me. "How what?"

"How are you going to make it up to me?"

"I don't know, JT? What do you want me to do?"

"You can stop being so horrible to Helen."

She doesn't even deem to look at me. "Why on earth would I do that?"

"Because she's my friend."

"Well, that's your problem. What does it have to do with me?"

"Because I'm asking you."

"Not going to happen."

"So, you refuse to do one simple thing for me after all the shit you put me through this past week?"

We turn into the parking lot and she almost runs a couple of girls over while pulling into a space. She turns to me, barely able to hold back her anger and frustration. "I don't like Helen. I never will. She's a lying, blackmailing bitch. She thinks she's fucking perfect, but she's not. What don't you get about that, JT?" She yanks her purse off the back seat and glares at me. "As for all the *shit* I put you through last week, it's over. You're done with your suspension and you survived. You didn't die, so can we please move on?"

"That's it? I'm done and I didn't die, so move on?"

"What do you want from me, JT? How am I supposed to make it up to you if I don't know what you want? Tell me and I'll do it."

"I already told you what I want."

She opens her door and glares at me. "And I told you that's not going to happen." She slams the door and stomps off across the grass to the front of the school. I get out and let her get a good distance ahead of me. Helen pulls in a few spaces down, but I don't wait for her. There's somebody else I need to talk to.

TWENTY-FOUR
AN HOUR LATER ON FRIDAY

I GET lots of abuse as soon as I walk into homeroom. Suddenly everyone is a comedian. I ignore it because Trish is sitting in her chair, doodling Miles' name on her notebook cover. I grab the seat next to her and lean in close, invading her personal space. Her eyelashes are ridiculously long and feathery. Maddie says they're mink hair extensions. Who thinks of this stuff? She gives me a shove. "Go away, JT."

"Come, Trish, where's the love? Aren't you glad to see me back in homeroom after a week? I have a question for you."

She looks at me sideways. "If I answer it, will you go away?" Her perfume smells like vanilla, but she's got coffee breath, so I back up a little.

"Only if you tell me the truth."

She squints at me and thinks for a second. "Whatever."

"Maddie called Helen a blackmailing bitch. I want to know what she did to blackmail Maddie."

She looks away from me. "I don't know what you're talking about."

I give her a little poke on the shoulder and she shrugs me off. "Oh, please, don't lie to me. Maddie tells you everything."

"No, she doesn't. Besides, she'll kill me."

"Come on, I know you know what happened. Just tell me. I won't say anything to Maddie."

She stares at me for a couple of seconds and goes back to doodling. "I can't. She'll kill me."

I'm so frustrated that I almost think about blackmailing her. I know plenty of secrets that Trish would never want Miles to know, but then I'd be as bad as her and Maddie. I push the chair back to where I found it. "Thanks, Trish. Good to know who my friends are."

I go back to my seat and the homeroom teacher quiets us down for morning announcements. A few minutes later the intercom buzzes and the teacher answers and looks at directly at me. What now?

"JT, Mr. Serrano wants you to stop by his office before first period. You can go now."

Shit. He couldn't know anything. There's no way he saw me last night and Helen isn't meeting with Ms. Deon until later. I grab my stuff and make my way down the hall to the math department. All the math teachers share a room, but Mr. Serrano has a small office for himself because he's the department head.

The door is open but I knock on the jamb to get his attention. He tells me to close the door and points to the chair across from his desk. Mr. Serrano reaches below his desk and pulls out a plastic grocery store bag. He turns it over and dumps a soggy, half-eaten left shoe in front of me. My crossword puzzle Vans are no more. I can see where Maddie filled in our names in the blank spaces. Hers is 14 across and mine is 21 down. I don't look up.

haven't learned anything. Not from Ms. McKay, not from Jackie Thompson, and not from Helen last year."

Her face gets dark with anger. "I told you I had nothing to do with your precious Helen last year. That was somebody else."

I hold up the camera by its sparkly strap. "No, Maddie, it was you. The proof is on this camera. You lied to me when we first started going out and it hasn't gotten any better since then."

Her face goes completely pale and she looks at Trish, panicked. She says, "You were supposed to delete those."

Trish says back, "It's your camera. *You* were supposed to delete them."

"Why did you do that to Helen, Maddie? What did she ever do to you?"

She looks at me, her eyes flashing with anger. "Because I can't stand her. She's a know-it-all bitch that's always in everybody's face about something. She deserved it."

"Nobody deserves to be humiliated in front of the whole school, Maddie."

"That was last year, JT. It's over, for God's sake. Why are you even bringing it up?"

"Because it's not over, Maddie. It's not over for Helen. It's not over for all the kids that still call her Mosquito Bites. Things aren't over just because you want them to be. It doesn't work that way."

"Well, this conversation is over, JT. Give me my camera so I can leave."

"Fine, I'm done, anyway. I'm done protecting you. I'm done looking the other way. I'm done with you." I give her a second to say something, but she doesn't, so I toss the camera to her and I start to walk away. Maddie grabs my arm and says, "You aren't going to tell Deon about the tweet, are you? I'm just saying because you can't prove it was me."

I shake my head. "No. I don't care about the stupid tweet anymore. Maybe you should do yourself a favor and stay off the internet for a while. It just brings out the horrible in you."

She glares at me and shoves the camera in her purse. She barks at Trish to get in the car, but Trish shakes her head and says, "I'm taking the bus."

Maddie glares at her. "Whatever. Fuck both of you." She slams her door and backs out of the parking space with a squeal of tires.

Trish looks at me and says, "Do you still want to know why Helen was blackmailing Maddie?" I nod my head and she steps closer. "This didn't come from me, OK? Promise you won't tell Maddie?"

"I don't think we'll be talking any time soon, but I promise."

She looks over her shoulder to make sure the Volvo is nowhere in sight. "Maddie was still seeing her old boyfriend when you guys started dating and Helen found out. She told Maddie to that she was going to tell you if she didn't break it off with one of you."

I wasn't expecting that. Trish reads the shock on my face. "Sorry, but you asked."

Maddie told me that she hadn't dated anybody for three months when I asked her out. "How long?"

She shrugs her shoulders. "I don't know, maybe a month."

"A month?"

"Yeah, I think. He goes to some prep school but he comes home on weekends. You promise you won't tell her I told you?"

I nod my head. "I promise."

I start to leave, but she grabs my arm and leans in close. "She was with him again, last Saturday, when you couldn't go out. And she didn't go to her uncle's house on Sunday. She spent the day with him. I'm really sorry, JT."

My face flushes with heat. That's why she was so evasive. I start to ask who he is, but I change my mind. I don't even care. "Thanks, Trish. I won't say anything."

I check my phone for the time. Damn, I'm late for track practice. If I run, maybe I can be on the track before the coach notices. I dodge kids in the courtyard and slip through the front doors, but before I can make it down the hallway, I hear somebody calling my name. I turn and spot Ms. Deon waving at me. Crap.

"JT, I need a minute of your time, if you don't mind."

"Um, I'm kind of late for practice and Coach is already mad at me, so I kind of need to go. How about if we do this on Monday?"

"I'll write you a note. Come with me, please."

I shove my hands in my pockets and jam my finger on the memory card from Maddie's camera. A dark thought comes into my mind. Maybe Ms. Deon would like to see some photos while we chat. I follow her into her office and take a seat facing the courtyard. Ms. Deon pulls my folder out of a drawer and I notice it's gotten thicker since I was last in here. This can't be good.

"I've become aware that certain letters were sent to Stanford this week."

I don't know what to say, but she keeps looking at me, so I know I'm supposed to respond somehow. "Yeah, I guess I can kiss my acceptance and scholarship goodbye."

She arches her eyebrows at me. "That's it. You're going to give up without a fight?"

"What am I supposed to do? It's their word against mine."

"But Stanford doesn't know what your word is, do they?"

I stare back at her. She's right. They don't know my side of the story. "Do you think they'd even listen?"

She shrugs her shoulders. "I would."

"But I have no idea what I would say."

"I usually start from the beginning and see where it takes me. I recommend that you work on it this weekend and run it by me on Monday. I've come across these situations before and I might be able to help you present a good argument."

I'm completely shocked. She's willing to help me save my butt? "I can do that. I'll have a letter first thing, Monday. I'll even use spell-check."

She laughs and says, "Always a good idea, JT. Now, let me write you a note."

I stand up and finger the memory card while she writes out the note and seals it in an envelope. "Ms. Deon, I have a question." She hands me the envelope and arches her eyebrows, telling me to go ahead. "What if you had proof that somebody did something really bad, but it was a while ago and bringing it up would hurt the person that was hurt in the first place all over again?"

She looks at me for a few seconds before she answers. "I'd need to know more specifics. If a crime was committed and you're withholding evidence, then that's a serious situation."

I have to think about that. "What if it wasn't really a crime, but just something mean? You know?"

"Then I'd ask myself what I wanted to achieve. Is wanting the person who was mean to be punished more important than possibly hurting somebody else? If it's something that know that. He just strung you along, messing with you until he got what he needed. But what you did was huge. You stood up for something you believed in and you made a difference. Remember the righteous thrill of nailing Serrano's sorry ass while you were clinging to that tree and that dog was eating your shoe and you didn't know if you'd make it out alive? That was your transformation. That was the moment you went from being Maddie's boyfriend to being a real person. You defined yourself. You're not a hollow chocolate bunny anymore. Congratulations."

She stands up and gives me a military salute. "I have to get to calculus, but my guess is we won't be having class today. See you around, John Taylor. Enjoy your newfound cojones."

happened a long time ago, maybe the victim has moved on and doesn't want to revisit the situation."

"What if the mean person is still being mean and might hurt somebody else?"

She shakes her head. "I don't know, JT. If you want to tell me the specifics, I can be of more help. Right now, it sounds like you might need to do some more thinking on the matter."

I nod my head and slip the envelope into my back pocket. "You're right, maybe I need to think about it some more." I stop at the door and turn around. "Thanks, for offering to help with Stanford and everything."

"I suggest you spend a long time working on that letter."

I smile at her. "I'm grounded. I have all weekend to make it perfect."

I wait until I get down the hall before I start running. It's like a weight's been lifted off me and I can move again. Serrano sucks big-time for sending that letter, but I get the last word. I swoop past kids straggling down to the locker rooms, cutting around boys and running backwards to check out a group of girls slow-walking down the hall. Three of them run track so I yell at them to get their butts in gear or they'll be late. When I get to the end of the hall, I take a skidding left and almost crash into Coach as he comes out of the locker room. So much for sneaking past him.

TWENTY-SEVEN
FRIDAY, AFTER SCHOOL

THE LATE BUS drops me off at the center of town, a couple of blocks from my house. It's so beautiful out that I take the long way home, around the town common and the old stables and down to the basketball courts. Some little kids are shooting hoops so I stop and watch them play. Helen and I must have played a million games of HORSE here. She had a mean spin shot that I could never copy. I had to change the rules so she couldn't use it more than once per game.

After a couple of minutes, I keep walking and cross the intersection to my street. Helen is sitting on her front steps, talking to her Auntie Lin, so I make my way over to say hello.

Lin gives me a big smile. "John Taylor, we meet again." Her t-shirt says, "*Yes my boobs are fake, my real ones tried to kill me.*" Now I know where Helen gets her t-shirt supply.

I look in the driveway for her car. "You still have the Mustang? Cool."

"Yeah, I only use it on nice days now. I've got too many miles on it for every-day driving." She squints up at the sky.

"Speaking of nice days, I have to get out of the sun. This damn chemo makes me burn up in no time."

Helen stands up and brushes off her butt. "You want to come in? We'll try not to embarrass you too much."

I shake my head. "Can I talk to you for a minute?"

She gives me a worried look. "You're not still mad at me, are you? Should I have Lin stick around to protect me?"

"No, I've recovered. You won't need your bodyguard."

Auntie Lin gives me a hug and says, "In that case, I'll wait inside. Good to see you, JT. Don't be a stranger."

Helen sits back down on the steps and I drop down next to her. She says, "How was track practice?"

"Brutal. I was late and the team lost yesterday because I wasn't at the meet. Coach made me do twice as much as everybody else."

"Why were you late? Out frolicking in the sunshine with Maddie?"

"No, I had some business to take care of." I try to think of the best way to tell her I'm sorry, tell her I was a jerk for not believing her, but I don't have the words. I pull the memory card out of my pocket. "Here, I thought maybe you'd want this."

She holds it up and looks at me. "Um, thanks, JT. Flowers or jewelry I can see, but an old memory card...I'm not sure I'm ready for this level of commitment." Why does she always have to be a wise-ass?

"It's got some pictures on it. I'm pretty sure they're the only copies. I figured you'd know how dispose of them properly."

Helen closes her fist around the card and looks away. When she looks back at me, her cheeks are wet with tears. "Where did you get this?"

"Little pink camera. Maddie thought she had deleted them."

She snuffles her nose and stares at the blue plastic square. "You know, every day I check the internet expecting to find these posted somewhere. It's like she stole part of me and wouldn't give it back. This really means a lot to me, JT. I don't know how I'm going to thank you."

"Don't worry about it. I figure it's the least I can do for a friend, right?"

She pulls her black skull bandanna out of her pocket and wipes her face off. "Does Maddie know you found these?"

"Yeah, she knows."

"I'm guessing she's not very happy with you right now."

I shrug my shoulders. "I know she's not. It doesn't matter because I told her we're done."

"Really? You broke up with her over this?"

"Not just that. Everything. She lied to me about a lot of stuff. Like you told me more than once, she's not exactly the nicest person when you look closely." I have to stop for a second to find the right words. "But those photos, they were the main reason. I'm sorry. I never should have doubted you."

"I'm sorry, too. I wrote you off. I never should have done that." She smacks me on the knee. "Wait a minute, when you found the photos, you didn't look, did you? Because they weren't exactly flattering."

"No, of course not." Time to change the subject. "I talked to Ms. Deon. She knows about Serrano's email and she thinks I should tell Stanford my side of the story. She even offered to help with the letter."

Helen nods. "Ms. Deon's cool. You should definitely take her up on her offer." She slaps me on my leg again. "That reminds me, we don't have to worry about seeing Serrano or

McKay next week. They've both been suspended without pay until the school board hearing this summer. And, since everybody in our class has already taken the AP Calc exam, we get a free period for the rest of the year. Cool, huh?"

I let out a sigh. "Definitely. I was not looking forward running into Serrano on Monday."

She folds the bandanna into a square and lays it flat on her thigh, tracing the patterns with her finger. "Did you really break up with Maddie? Are you going to be OK? I mean you seemed like you were really in pretty deep, there. Well, with Maddie, ankle-high is deep, but you know what I mean."

I flick an ant off my shoe. "I don't know. To be honest, I was going to call it off before we went to college. She's not really the long-distance type, or the short distance type for that matter." I watch her expression. "She was cheating on me again. I suppose you knew that, too."

Her eyes narrow. "Really? Again? That weasel! Want me to take her out? We're playing softball in PE. I could make it look like an accident."

"No, thanks for the offer, but I think I'll pass. I'm not really the sociopathic revenge type of guy."

"OK, just let me know if you change your mind. I'm thinking one shot to the mouth and she'd have dinner plates for lips just in time for graduation pictures."

The day is too nice to go inside, so I sit with Helen and watch the kids from the basketball court walk past us. I notice her hair is starting to grow back. She hasn't shaved in a few days. I give her a nudge with my elbow. "You're getting kind of shaggy, there. You run out of razor blades?"

"No, I'm growing it out. I don't want to look like a total psycho when I get to college." She stands up and stretches.

"You want to come inside? Lin and I are planning our trip to California. The invitation to join us is still open."

I shrug my shoulders. "I don't want to impose."

"Come on, you're going to pass up the opportunity to drive across the country with two weird, bald chicks in a turd-brown Vanagon? We're going to visit the birthplace of JELL-O and the Spam Museum. It's going to be awesome."

She holds her hand out and I let her pull me up. "Well, you didn't say there was going to be JELL-O. That changes everything."

END

ACKNOWLEDGMENTS

I want to thank my wife, Karen, who patiently listens to me when I try to work out the details of my stories and who more than once has helped me solve a complex problem with a simple answer.

I also want to thank my critique group in order of seniority, but not importance: Erin Dionne, Phoebe Sinclair, Megan Mullin, Annette Trossello, Wendy McDonald, and Danielle Renino. Without them, I'd still be stuck on a story about a little girl and a dog that went absolutely nowhere. I count on them to always bring their individual perspectives along with honest, constructive feedback. Thanks for helping me to become a better writer.

ABOUT THE AUTHOR

Although G. J. Crespo moved a lot while growing up, he spent most of middle school and high school in a small town in central Massachusetts.

When not writing, he spends his time cooking, reading, and learning about his family's Irish and Puerto Rican roots.

He lives north of Boston with his wife and an extremely handsome Ragdoll cat.

While he is not a math genius, he is mildly obsessed with numbers (just a small sample of the things he counts: he is one of *seven* children, he has owned *eight* cars, he went to *nine* different schools before graduating, he coached his daughter's soccer team for *ten* years, and he has *eleven* nieces and nephews).

www.ingramcontent.com/pod-product-compliance
Lightning Source LLC
LaVergne TN
LVHW091548060526
838200LV00036B/743

TWENTY-SIX
FRIDAY AFTERNOON

I DON'T GO to the library. I stay on the stone wall and try to figure out what comes next. Helen is *so* screwed up. This wasn't one of her stupid causes. There weren't any t-shirts to wear or posters to hang up. Deep down at the root of everything, it was just me trying desperately to save my ass. It wasn't about bringing Serrano or McKay down, it was about getting the hell out of this stupid town and never coming back.

Now I'm stuck here. Serrano won. He took me down. Maddie won. She's going to graduate and get her new car and go to UMASS with Trish they'll get drunk and be horrible to people while I stay home and take care of Mamo and work at Cumberland Farms.

I pull Maddie's camera out of my pocket and turn it on. I scroll through the photos until I get to the pictures I saw this morning. I still can't believe it was her. I turn the camera off and stuff it in my pocket. I still have one hand left to play.

I wait for Maddie at her car after school. She and Trish come strolling across the lawn together. I put on my best happy face and smile at both of them. I can see the relief on Maddie's face.

Maddie says, "Why aren't you at track practice?"

"I'm on my way, I just wanted to talk to you for a minute." Trish waits a short distance away, close enough to hear what we're saying, but not close enough to be obvious that she's eavesdropping.

I lean against the fender of her car and pull Maddie's camera out of my pocket. "Thanks for lending me your camera. It was very educational."

Maddie furrows her brows at me and says, "What's that supposed to mean?"

"It means I learned a lot when I went through the old photos on it. There were three in particular that I found very interesting."

She tries to grab the camera out of my hand, but I hold it out of her reach. "What are you talking about?"

"You lied to me and I believed you. I stood up for you and I hurt somebody that I care about. I can't believe I was so clueless."

Trish says, "Maybe I should go. I can still catch the bus before it leaves."

Maddie turns to her and says, "No, Trish, you can stay. JT has to get going anyway." She turns back to me, her anger clearly coming up. "Why were you going through my photos? That's like invading my privacy. That is *so* wrong, JT."

"No, Maddie, what's so wrong is the way you treat people. You can't go around being horrible to people and get away with it. I'm tired of looking the other way because despite all the trouble you've caused and all the people you've hurt, you

Mr. Serrano says, "I found my dog Skipper chewing on this when I was leaving for work this morning. Does it look familiar to you?"

I don't say anything. He knows it's mine.

"I can only assume it was you that he treed last night, not a raccoon. I'm curious. What were you doing at my house in the middle of a thunderstorm?"

I look him in the eye. "I know that the file I downloaded for you had the answers to the state exam on it. I saw you and Ms. McKay changing the answers last night. All your lectures about being a decent person are complete bullshit. You cheated on the state exams."

"And do you have any proof of these accusations? Anything to back them up?"

I lie to him. I don't want him going after Helen. "No."

"Did you keep a copy of the files you downloaded?"

"No."

"So, it's your word against mine. A student that was suspended for harassing a math teacher versus the head of the math department. A student who was trespassing on private property in the middle of the night versus the school's Teacher of the Year for the third year in a row. Tell me Mr. Monahan, why would anybody ever believe you over me?"

I stare at him. "Why is it OK for you to do something wrong, but when I make one mistake, you want to ruin my life?"

"Because I'm acting on behalf of the school. What I did will get us more funding and will improve our ranking in the state. More students will come here instead of going to private schools. My actions are for the good of all, yours were selfish and benefited nobody."

This guy is a total bastard. He actually thinks the rules don't apply to him.

"Ms. McKay still sucks. She's a shit teacher today and she'll still be shit next year."

His face clouds over and that twitching eye gets worse. "And you'll be enjoying a fine education at a local community college or trade school rather than attending Stanford. You see, I knew you were beyond redemption. Your actions last night just proved I was right. As a result, I'm more than delighted to tell you that I sent that letter out yesterday morning. And by the way, Ms. McKay sent a similar letter as well."

The blood drains from my face. "You said you were going to wait to see how the kids did on the test."

Mr. Serrano smiles his Indian corn smile at me and says, "Actually, most of them did much better than we thought they would. It made my job last night a little easier." He stands up and holds the door open for me. "You should run along now. Don't want to be late for your classes."

I barely make it to physics by the late bell. I sit down a couple of seats away Helen and she knows immediately that something's wrong. She leans forward in her seat and catches my eye and mouths, "What?"

I shake my head. This is not the place. I mouth back. "Later."

TWENTY-FIVE
STILL FRIDAY MORNING

HELEN YANKS me into an empty classroom as soon as physics is over.

"Spill it, JT. What's going on?"

I take a deep breath. Why am I shaking? Why am I fighting back tears?

She says, "What is it? Serrano? Maddie? What's the matter?"

I force myself to breath normally. "Serrano found my shoe. He knows that I know that he cheated."

"Did you tell him about the photos?"

"No, he doesn't have a clue." I take another breath. "He sent the letter out. He fucking sent it out yesterday."

"No way. To Stanford?"

"Yes, and McKay sent one, too. I'm screwed. I'm completely and utterly screwed."

Helen stares at the ground, thinking, then she reaches up and grabs me by the shoulders. "I'll see what I can do."

"What can you possibly do? It doesn't matter what happens

with Deon and the state test guy. The letters already went out. Stanford is probably already ripping up my acceptance letter. What don't you get about this? I'm screwed beyond all possible salvation. Fucking bastard. I'm going to go kick his pompous, lying, cheating ass."

Helen grabs me by the shirt and says, "JT, chill out already. I got this. I got your back. I won't let Serrano screw you over, OK? You have to trust me."

I do trust her, but how can she possibly fix this? "What are you going to do?"

She smiles and pats me on the cheek. "I have a few tricks up my sleeve. Serrano won't know what hit him. Now, we have a test to take. Clear your head and let's go kick some world history ass."

I take the test on autopilot. I have no idea how well I do, just that I finish seconds before the bell rings. The next class is a blurry, greasy smudge on my memory. I remember that Helen is there as she always is, but the teacher speaks in hieroglyphics and I didn't bring my Rosetta Stone to do the translation.

Helen catches my eye before she heads down to Deon's office and I meet her in the hallway. She says, "Can I trust you to remain calm until I see you at lunch? No hysterics, no meltdowns?"

I nod my head and mutter, "Whatever," so gives me a pinch on the back of my arm. It feels like a bee sting. I yank my arm away. "What did you do that for?"

"Get your shit together, JT. No moping allowed. Meet me outside the cafeteria at lunch, OK?"

When the bell rings for lunch, I dump my books in my locker and wait outside the cafeteria for Helen to show up. I'm not hungry, but I look in anyway. I see Maddie waiting in the salad line, but I'm not ready to deal with her just yet. I turn around and almost crash into Helen coming out of the girl's bathroom.

She says, "Just the person I was looking for."

I check her face for some sign of her mood, but she's totally neutral. "Let's go to the courtyard. We can have a little more privacy there."

I follow her out and we sit on the low wall by the front of the school. Technically, we're not supposed to hang out here, but Helen seems to know when and where she can bend the rules. I close my eyes and soak up the sun.

I ask her, "How did it go? Did you convince the jury of your innocence?"

Helen says, "I'll get to that in a minute. We never really talked about last night. How did you get the photos? I want details."

"It was a total disaster. Possibly the worst night of my life." I tell her about the rain and mud and Skipper and my shoe and how I peed on Skipper's head and she's laughing so hard there are tears running down her cheeks.

She catches her breath and looks at me. "I can't believe you went to all that trouble to get those blurry photos. Any normal kid could have bailed as soon as they saw the dog."

I look at her. "I couldn't. I needed proof. I needed to get you off the hook."

"Why, because you were afraid I'd kill you in your sleep?"

I think about it for a second. "No, because it was the right thing to do. You didn't deserve to get in trouble because I was covering for Maddie."

Helen gives me a nudge with her elbow. "Maddie didn't deserve you covering for her either."

I don't say anything. There's nothing I can do about that now. The bell rings and I bump her with my elbow. "You're going to be late for calculus and I'm supposed to be in the library. We should probably get going."

I stand up and offer her my hand, but she pats the wall next her and says, "Sit back down, John Taylor, there's something you should see."

She points to the windows along the courtyard and I realize we can see right into Ms. Deon's office. Mr. Serrano and Ms. McKay are sitting at the conference table, talking to Ms. Deon and two guys in suits. My stomach does a back flip and I look at Helen. She smiles and says, "Don't worry, they're not talking about you. Well, you'll probably come up in the conversation, but you're cool. Nobody is going to drag you away in handcuffs."

She leans into me and says, "The guy on the right is the head of the state testing board, and the guy on the left, with the bad comb-over, is the superintendent of the school district."

"What are they doing here? How did they know about Serrano and McKay?"

She smiles at me. "There's a little something I didn't tell you. You know that big honkin' file I downloaded for you? The one that was password protected? Well, I broke into it and saw that it had all the answers to the sophomore math test. Being the trusting soul that I am, I figured Serrano had *you* download the files so they couldn't be traced to him. So, just in case he was up to no good, I used a little computer magic to alter the files so some of the answers were wrong, then I put it all back together before I gave you the flash drive. I figured that if he cheated, then he'd screw things up worse rather than fixing them."

My jaw drops. "You mean the file I gave to Serrano was altered."

"Affirmative."

"But, the state test guys traced the download to you and they called you in?"

She does a little snorting laugh. "No, they didn't have a clue."

I shake my head, trying to make sense of what she's saying. "How did you get called into Ms. Deon's office about the download?"

"Isn't it obvious?"

"Um, no."

"Jeez, JT, think about it. Ms. Deon called me into her office because I was her prime suspect for my little balloon prank. She didn't have definitive proof, but I was on my fifteenth strike and facing suspension, so I made a plea deal. I tell her about a certain cheating scandal and she forgets about the pink balloon."

"You ratted out Serrano to get off the hook for your prank?"

"Yeah, I would have left an anonymous tip anyway, but why not use it to keep myself out of trouble?" She looks over at the conference room and smiles. When I look up, Serrano is glaring at us, murderous thoughts clearly in his eyes.

Helen turns back to me. "Anyway, Ms. Deon contacted the testing board with my information and they traced the files to some disgruntled programmer that was looking to make a little money by selling the answers. He confessed that he met Serrano at a teacher conference and gave him the download info. We just needed to sit back and wait for him to use them."

"You mean with the screwed-up answers?"

"Yup. The tests were picked up first thing this morning and they went right to the pages I changed and sure enough, thirty-two tests had been altered to match the wrong answers. They didn't even mix them in with the others, they left them on the top of the pile."

"Wait, this was all going on behind the scenes and you knew about it?"

"Well, yeah."

I stare at her, slack-jawed and blinking in disbelief. "So, you were never really in trouble with the test police? They weren't tracking your downloads? You weren't going to cheating jail? I didn't have to get soaked and chased and have a stupid dog eat my shoe?"

She seems surprised that I'm mad. "Well, technically, no, but the photos did help seal the deal."

"I can't believe this. You lied to me. Jesus, I can't trust anybody."

"Well, if you want to get picky about things then yes, I did stretch the truth a little. But aren't you psyched that I did? You would have missed out on all the fun if I didn't."

"You're insane, you know that? You have gone off the deep end."

"Why are you being so negative about this? I inspired you to greatness, JT. You said you did it because it was the right thing to do. You helped bring down a tyrant. You put yourself out on a limb and proved that Serrano and McKay were cheating, pun intended. You should be proud of yourself. Doesn't it feel awesome?"

"Not really, Serrano still screwed me over. He sent the letter out and I'm stuck in Appleton the rest of my life."

"Serrano was going to send that letter no matter what. You